He was spying on her.

He'd hired people to watch her. "Why?"

Finn leaned against the porch, and Genevieve couldn't stop noticing his hands or remembering how they could make her feel. The pleasure and excitement.

"Because you matter to me."

She wanted to tear her gaze away and regain control. But she couldn't. His gaze was magnetic.

"I know I hurt you, Genni, but I realize now—"

"You're just saying that because I'm the first woman who's ever told you no. The first one to resist."

A flash of something crossed his face and before she could react, Finn had her flush against him.

"Don't lie, Genni. We both know you can't resist if I seduce you."

Her mouth opened in protest, but her brain shut down the words before they could leave her lips. Because no matter how she tried to deny it, he was right.

* * *

The Devil's Bargain by Kira Sinclair is part of the Bad Billionaires series.

Dear Reader,

Isn't it fun to break the rules sometimes? To walk on the wild side now and again? To do something that makes you feel alive? While two of the men in my Bad Billionaires series would disagree, Finn DeLuca wholeheartedly embraces the idea that rules are simply suggestions. Sure, he doesn't have a traditional moral compass, but he definitely has his own set of rules that govern his life and choices. To the outside world, he might appear nothing more than an opportunistic criminal. Good thing Genevieve Reilly can see beneath the well-crafted facade to the pain, fear and need Finn is desperate to hide.

Genevieve Reilly wants nothing to do with Finn DeLuca. Unfortunately, their shared son means she doesn't have much of a choice but to confront him and the past that changed the trajectory of her life. However, with each encounter, she learns a little more about who Finn truly is and not just who he wants the world to see. The question is, can she ever learn to trust him...and her own compromised judgment?

Writing this story allowed me to take a precarious walk on the wild side, and I hope reading it gives you the chance to do the same. Enjoy the ride as you read Finn and Genevieve's story! I'd love to hear from you at www.kirasinclair.com or come chat with me on Twitter at www.Twitter.com/kirasinclair. And don't forget to check out the other Bad Billionaires novels coming soon!

Best wishes,

Kira

KIRA SINCLAIR

THE DEVIL'S BARGAIN

DESIRE

Recycling programs
for this product may
not exist in your area.

ISBN-13: 978-1-335-20941-2

The Devil's Bargain

Copyright © 2020 by Kira Bazzel

This edition published by arrangement with Harlequin Books S.A.

For questions and comments about the quality of this book, please contact us at CustomerService@Harlequin.com.

Harlequin Enterprises ULC
22 Adelaide St. West, 40th Floor
Toronto, Ontario M5H 4E3, Canada
www.Harlequin.com

Printed in U.S.A.

Kira Sinclair's first foray into writing romance was for a high school English assignment, and not even being forced to read the Scotland-set historical aloud to the class could dampen her enthusiasm...although it definitely made her blush. She sold her first book to Harlequin Blaze in 2007 and has enjoyed exploring relationships, falling in love and happily-ever-afters since. She lives in North Alabama with her two teenage daughters and their ever-entertaining bernedoodle puppy, Sadie. Kira loves to hear from readers at Kira@KiraSinclair.com.

Books by Kira Sinclair

Harlequin Desire

Bad Billionaires

The Rebel's Redemption
The Devil's Bargain

Harlequin Blaze

The Risk-Taker
She's No Angel
The Devil She Knows
Captivate Me
Testing the Limits
Bring Me to Life
Handle Me
Rescue Me

Visit her Author Profile page at Harlequin.com, or kirasinclair.com, for more titles.

You can also find Kira Sinclair on Facebook, along with other Harlequin Desire authors, at Facebook.com/harlequindesireauthors!

Family is everything.
Over the years, my daughters have given me constant encouragement, purpose, unconditional love and support. Angel and Sunshine, this one is for you. I love you both! (And I'll ignore the fact that the dirty dishes are still in the sink.) ♥

One

Three years. That's how long she'd successfully avoided Finn DeLuca. Apparently, the reprieve was over.

Genevieve Reilly stared at her attorney...waiting for him to laugh. Or tell her April fool. Or pinch her so she'd finally wake up.

"At least the judge recognized the validity of our argument against letting him take Noah overnight."

Oh, because that was the silver lining in this nightmare.

"How? How could this happen? You promised me he'd never be granted visitation. He's a convicted felon, for God's sake."

"No." Lance reached across the conference table and placed a soothing hand on her arm. "I told you it wasn't likely. But it appears Mr. DeLuca has not only influence of his own, but also friends in high places. Anderson Stone spoke on his behalf as a character witness."

"Another convicted felon."

"With billions of dollars and a media campaign touting him as a hero who saved the love of his life from a rapist."

"Whoop-dee-do. That has nothing to do with Finn. Finn isn't a hero. In fact, I'm pretty sure he's the devil's son."

Genevieve rubbed at the ache lodged right between her eyes. She'd regret the day she ever met Finn De-Luca…except that would mean she'd have to regret her son. And nothing could ever make that happen. Noah was the best thing in her life.

Having Noah had given her the strength to walk away from a life that was slowly poisoning her. Yes, the decision meant she and Noah had to fight for everything they had…but the fight was worth it. She'd do without if it meant raising her son in an environment that was healthy and happy.

Lance shrugged his shoulders. "Devil or not, he's Noah's father. And let's be honest, he has enough money that he could have fought us as long as he wanted."

That had sorta been her hope…and also what had kept her up at night. As long as they were in a court battle, then she didn't have to face him. But she didn't have access to unlimited bank accounts anymore so paying for all those legal bills would have been difficult. She'd have managed. Somehow.

They could appeal the judge's decision, but in the meantime Finn would get visitation. Which meant she'd

have to see him. A reality she'd been both dreading…
and dreaming about.

Waking up with her sex throbbing from memories
of Finn was something she tried not to think about. She
didn't really want him. Couldn't, wouldn't let herself.

Nope, she refused to admit that any part of her
wanted to see Finn DeLuca again.

Her last memory of him had been less than happy.
Blue-and-red lights reflecting off the forecourt of her
grandfather's estate. The cool, remote expression on
Finn's face as an officer placed a hand to the top of his
head and guided him into the back seat of the cruiser.

She'd refused to attend his trial. There'd been no
point. And, thank God, the prosecutor hadn't needed her
to testify. Not when Finn had been caught red-handed
with a fifteen-million-dollar diamond stuffed in his
pocket.

Her diamond. Or, rather, her family's. Nearly losing
the Star of Reilly to the charismatic, smooth-talking
devil had almost gotten her disowned…a fate Genevieve had spent her entire life bending over backward
to avoid. It was the threat her grandfather had used to
keep her in line from the time she was very young.

After losing her parents at an early age, her grandfather had been the only family she'd ever known. He
might have been the monster in her closet, but he was
all she had. So she'd grown up desperate to please him.
Desperate not to lose him, too.

Who knew a few months after Finn's arrest she'd be
the one walking away? Life was funny…and not for the
faint of heart.

And the thought of seeing Finn again had Genevieve's stomach flipping uncomfortably close to her throat. He was handsome, charismatic, dynamic and dangerous. He was temptation personified, and despite everything, Genevieve didn't exactly trust herself to hate him. Even if she should.

"Mr. DeLuca's attorney has requested you provide your preferred location for the visit. He expressed his client's desire for you to be comfortable."

Well, wasn't that just dandy? And not a thing like the Finn she knew. The man she remembered had been selfish and self-centered. Generous to a fault with those around him, but only because being charming was innate, not because he gave a damn about anyone else. Even now, she'd bet everything she owned that his generosity had nothing to do with Genevieve's comfort.

Finn DeLuca wanted something—something more than access to her son. She just hadn't figured out what. Yet.

At least she could guarantee he no longer wanted to use her for her access to the Reilly estate. He had to be aware of her change in circumstances. In fact, the tiny shreds of the check he'd sent, which were sitting on top of her dresser, were proof that he knew her grandfather didn't support her anymore.

Like Finn could buy his way back into her life. Or Noah's life. She didn't need his money and wouldn't have taken it even if she had. Noah might not have boarding school in his future, but she could afford to provide for her son without Finn's tainted offering.

"Genevieve?"

Hell, this was really happening. She'd spent the last couple months hoping this day wouldn't come. She'd refused to allow herself to contemplate the possibility that it might. So, she wasn't prepared.

"Tell him to come by my place Saturday morning. Ten o'clock. We'll figure out what to do from there. But he isn't taking my son anywhere without me. Not until I know for certain he's capable of caring for him and keeping him safe."

"I'm fairly certain Mr. DeLuca will agree to whatever you want."

That was a lie. Because if it were true, Finn would have respected her wishes and disappeared from her life for good.

Finn DeLuca stared at the file spread across the desk in front of him. His feet were kicked up onto the hard surface beside the eight-by-ten glossy of his son being pushed on one of those baby swings in the park.

He looked exactly like Finn's younger brother had at that age. Before everything went to hell.

Noah's pale blue eyes were alight with pure joy as wind ruffled his dirty-blond curls. His cheeks were chubby and pink and the perfect bow of his mouth was open on a peal of laughter.

This wasn't the first time Finn had seen the photograph. Or the first time he'd found himself staring at it, lost in a complex web of emotions he didn't have the experience to unravel.

He wasn't used to giving a damn about anything but himself.

But from the first time he'd seen a picture of his son—the one the hospital took when he'd been born—Finn had been lost.

No, that wasn't entirely true. He'd had a similar response the first time he'd laid eyes on Noah's mother. Genevieve…perplexed him. Enticed him in a way no one else ever had.

Unbidden, Finn's gaze traveled to the image of the woman standing behind Noah. Her arms were outstretched, waiting for the swing to return so she could push him again. Her flame-red hair had been pulled up into a tight knot at the top of her head, but the few strands that had fallen down were fluttering around her face.

He knew it was long…when she chose to let it down. Which was oh-so-rare. He could count on one hand the number of times he'd seen it in anything aside from a knot or a tail. And those few times had been because he'd asked her to leave it free.

He remembered running his fingers through the soft strands, reveling in the silky texture of it. Spreading it out across his pillow. The soft, blurred expression in her pale green eyes with the evergreen ring as his fingers played across her naked skin.

Dammit, he had to get control of himself. Sporting a half-hard erection at the mere thought of Genevieve's head on his pillow wasn't going to get him very far with her. In fact, it would have her building her walls even higher and faster.

And he needed her buy-in to have access to his son.

Shaking his head, Finn shuffled the photograph beneath the report he'd just been handed.

"Thanks, man. What do I owe you?"

Across the desk, Anderson Stone frowned at him, clearly perturbed at the question.

"Nothing. You know I'd do anything to help you. I'm just glad you're finally getting the chance to meet him. It's been a long six months."

It had been, but things were finally coming together. He might be reckless, but Finn had always understood the benefit of patience and laying the groundwork for success. Part of what he'd loved most about pulling off heists was the planning and anticipation.

Not to mention the adrenaline rush of triumph.

Running a finger over his lips, Finn sent his friend a chiding glance. "You know, the purpose of running a business is to make a profit."

"I'm aware," Stone drawled out.

"Apparently not, since I'm unaware of any other clients you're currently assisting. See, how it works is, when you provide services you request payment from those who benefit."

"Oh, is that how it works? Remind me, which one of us holds an MBA?"

Finn scoffed. "Just because I don't have an overpriced piece of paper with my name scrolled across it in fancy font doesn't mean I don't know what I'm talking about. Conversely, it doesn't make you an expert."

"I'm not hearing any complaints about the information you've been provided."

No, and he wouldn't complain. Finn was grateful for

everything Stone and Gray, the other leg in their tripod, had done for him.

Who would have expected them to go into business together? Opening Stone Surveillance had seemed unexpected when his friends had first told him they were going to do it. But once he began thinking…it made sense. Both of them had this drive to help people, a need to right wrongs.

Maybe because they'd both been wronged.

Finn, on the other hand, had never felt the need to assist anyone in his life. People got what they deserved. If they were stupid, they deserved to be taken advantage of. Then they could learn. The way he looked at it, any time he stole something pretty and valuable, he was providing a service. Highlighting the flaws in their security so they could correct the problem and prevent more loss.

If in the process he managed to acquire something he wanted…more the better.

The challenge was what drove him. Woe be it to anyone touting security that no one could break.

"You know we're not letting you pay, Finn. Besides, if you'd come on board like we asked months ago, then you'd be a full partner, anyway."

"Nope, thanks. I have a job."

Stone scoffed. "That isn't a job. When's the last time you stepped foot inside DeLuca Industries?"

"Uh…" Finn glanced up at the ceiling, seriously considering Stone's question. "Probably seven years ago, give or take six or seven months." His lips quirked into a self-deprecating smile. "They obviously don't need me. You know I review the quarterly financial and management reports. See, the key to running a successful business is hiring competent people to take care of it for you."

Stone shook his head. This was an argument they'd had many times over the last few years. His friend couldn't understand Finn's perspective because he came from a family that was entirely wrapped up in the day-to-day minutia of running the family business. Sure, that business was a multibillion-dollar corporation with a worldwide reach, but that didn't really change anything.

Finn, on the other hand, had decided early on that he wanted nothing to do with the family business. And felt not a single speck of guilt when he inherited it and handed it straight over to others to run.

Success and money afforded him the opportunity to do exactly as he pleased.

"Stealing things isn't a job, either."

Finn let a full-blown smile pull at his lips. "I haven't stolen a single thing, officer. At least, not since I've been out."

Stone scoffed. "Uh-huh. Is that because you've been preoccupied with Noah? I know you, Finn DeLuca. You're going to get bored. All I'm asking is that when it happens, don't do something stupid. I promise, we'll find a way to use your skills in a way that's beneficial to all of us…and keeps your ass outta jail."

Finn leaned back farther in his chair, tipping it onto the back two legs. Folding his hands behind his head, he enjoyed the sensation of being balanced on the edge…

just waiting for something to tip him one direction or the other.

The precipice was what called to him. The danger of walking on the brink. The potential of being caught was what made the rush so thrilling. Without it...

"Stone, I'm smart enough to keep myself out of jail. I've said it before, she's—" he gestured to the photograph beneath the pile of papers "—the only reason I got caught. I have no intention of ever letting that happen again."

Stone made a sound in the back of his throat that clearly stated his skepticism.

"I successfully pulled off more than two dozen jobs before her. I let myself get caught," Finn insisted.

"Uh-huh."

"I chose to go back. I put myself in that position."

Genevieve had distracted him. Made him sloppy. And he'd done something stupid. He had no intention of letting that happen again. What he needed right now was to win back Genevieve's trust so he could have access to his son. Period.

Stone's eyebrow rose, but he chose not to push him. Smart man. "Genevieve might be starting to make a splash on the jewelry scene, but her finances are precarious at best. What little money she got from her family is mostly tied up in inventory. Loose stones, precious metals."

His friend wasn't telling him anything Finn wasn't already aware of. He'd been going over Genevieve's financials just as closely as his own. He might ignore his company, but information was knowledge and he wouldn't let anyone take advantage of him.

What he didn't know was where Stone was going with this. "Your point?"

"She spent money she didn't have to hire a damn good lawyer to fight you."

Which was nothing less than what Finn had expected. And he hated to think of Genevieve putting herself and his son in that situation, but he'd remedy it as soon as possible.

"I tried to give her money. She hasn't cashed the check." Which also wasn't a surprise. But he had a plan to get her an influx of cash…one she couldn't afford to refuse. "Don't worry, man. I have everything under control."

Stone gave him a hard look. "I hope you know what you're doing."

Yeah, so did he.

Everything was riding on the next few weeks. One hiccup could cost him everything. But Finn was used to betting everything on a single well-planned adventure.

Genevieve paced through her living room, the heels of her shoes clicking against the hardwoods she'd refinished herself. Hands tucked beneath her crossed arms, she couldn't stop herself from looking out the open blinds to the street in front of her little house. Waiting.

Down the hall she could hear Maddie's happy, high-pitched voice as she read a book to Noah. She had no idea what she would have done over the last three years without her best friend. She'd been with Genevieve every step of the way…including being in the delivery room when Noah was born.

Maddie had also been there when Finn first slammed into Genevieve's life. There'd been something about him, something that drew Genevieve from the first moment they'd met, at a charity gala hosted by her grandfather.

Certainly, Finn was charismatic and handsome. Every female there that night had taken notice of him. But for Genevieve…it was more. She'd sensed the dangerous edge behind the polished exterior. And despite herself, she'd been tempted by it. For someone who'd been raised under a sheltered, strict upbringing that temptation had felt…deliciously forbidden. And so had he.

The sensual pull had only heightened when, without asking permission, he'd pulled her onto the dance floor. The warmth of his smooth palm caressed across her bare back. From that first encounter, she'd craved him.

Unfortunately, despite everything, there was a huge part of her that worried she still did.

Glancing at her watch, Genevieve felt her heart lurch into her throat. Five minutes.

What she couldn't understand was why Finn had fought so hard to meet Noah. The man she'd known had worked hard to avoid any semblance of responsibility to the point of outsourcing the management of his family's company. It wasn't likely he'd suddenly developed a burning desire to be a father.

Her biggest concern was the impact this was going to have on Noah. She really didn't want her son falling in love with his daddy only to have Finn disappear. Or disappoint. Both highly likely.

A car door slammed. Genevieve glanced at her watch again. Exactly ten. The chime on her front door pealed. Swallowing down the butterflies storming her belly, she stalked across the room to yank it open.

And lost her breath.

Damn him for being exactly as she remembered. His feet were spread, encased in large black motorcycle boots planted on the pale boards of her front porch. Shoulders packed with muscle, nearly as wide as her doorway, blocked her view of the car undoubtedly sitting at her curb. A perverse part of her wondered if he still drove the sleek Maserati he'd delighted in racing through the city at top speed, practically taunting the local police to pull him over.

He'd been reckless and wild. So different than she was, which was undoubtedly what had attracted her in the first place. Finn DeLuca was a force. A storm, beautiful and raging. Uncaring what he destroyed in his path.

His hair was just as dark, almost jet-black, and untamed as the rest of him. A thick scruff covered his chin and cheeks, giving the impression he couldn't be bothered to shave rather than he was cultivating an actual beard.

But it was his eyes that got to her. Every damn time. So dark they almost appeared black. But she'd been close enough to know they were actually a deep, dark shade of coffee brown. What had gotten her more than the color, though, was the way he'd looked at her…like he'd actually seen her. All of her, especially the pieces she'd gotten very good at hiding from everyone, including herself.

He'd been the devil sitting on her shoulder, tempting her to sin. With him, she'd felt powerful, intelligent and beautiful. He'd convinced her she could be daring, too.

Finn DeLuca had the uncanny ability to make her feel like she had no secrets…and that she didn't need any. Turns out he'd been right. She hadn't had any secrets from him because he'd researched every damn aspect of her life. And used each piece of knowledge against her. To make her care for him. Love him.

Trust him.

All so he could steal what he wanted—the Star of Reilly—without regard to the damage he inflicted on her life.

"The neighbors might start talking if you leave me standing on the front porch all day, Genni."

"Don't call me that." Her response was automatic. So was the way she stepped back, doing exactly what he'd wanted her to.

He paused beside her as he moved into her home. For a second she thought he was going to touch her. Genevieve tensed, not certain how she'd react. But instead of reaching out, Finn slowly turned his head and flashed her that dangerous, mischievous grin. The one that always made her knees go weak. Because whatever nefarious thought was usually behind that grin had inevitably left her a naked, quaking, pleasure-infused mess.

Nope, that wasn't happening now.

Shoving the door closed, Genevieve purposely

walked away from him. She stopped in the middle of her living room and swiveled, wrapping her arms around herself in a comforting hold.

"I don't know what you're hoping to gain here, Finn, but whatever it is, you can't have it."

"The only thing I want is the chance to get to know my son. You look real good, Genni."

She shook her head. "We both know that's not how you work, so cut the BS. I haven't figured out your play yet, but I will. And just in case you're not aware, although I'm sure you are, I no longer have access to the Reilly estate, including any of the jewels, the business or the art."

"Yep, I'm fully aware. Why do you think I wrote you that check?"

"Speaking of which, you can have the pieces back. And so we're clear, flattery won't get you anywhere with me. We both know you have the ability to spout pretty words with no substance. Don't waste your breath."

Finn's face drew tight. His mouth flattened into a sharp line, giving her an expression she'd never seen before. But that was probably because he'd only shown her what he wanted her to see.

"I meant what I said. And just so you know, I meant every word I've ever said to you. I might have done many things, but I never once lied to you."

Genevieve laughed, the sound of it very out of place. "Sure, except when you told me I could trust you and promised you'd never hurt me."

He took a single step toward her. Genevieve held up both hands.

"I'm sorry, Genevieve."

It was tempting to believe he actually meant the short declaration. She heard sincerity in the words. And there was a part of her that thought maybe he *was* sorry.

At least sorry he'd gotten caught.

"It doesn't matter anymore. I don't actually hate you, even though you deserve it. You gave me Noah. And even if it wasn't the way I would have preferred, you showed me I could have a life I didn't think possible. And gave me the confidence to fight for me and my son when I needed to. I'm happier now. But that doesn't mean I intend to forgive you or forget how you used and manipulated me."

It was Genevieve who closed the gap between them. She walked straight into his personal space, going toe-to-toe with him. She looked up into his dark, swarthy expression and said, "But I promise you this, I will never let you hurt or manipulate my son. So, for your sake, I hope you're telling me the truth. Because I'm not the naive, malleable girl you knew three years ago."

Two

Boy was she telling the truth.

Genevieve wasn't the innocent girl he'd known before. Back then he'd fought against the urge to protect and shelter her. To hurt her grandfather for the way he'd treated her. She'd been so meek. Beaten down by years of hearing she couldn't do anything right. Being constantly reminded of every mistake or flaw.

Even then Finn had known there was a fire deep inside her, banked and waiting for the right fuel to fan into something beautiful and mesmerizing.

He had been right.

The fierce expression in her gaze as she stared up at him made the blood whoosh faster in his veins. It made him want to grab her, yank her hard against him and devour that passion. And her soft, pink mouth.

But that would no doubt get him slapped.

And might cost him the opportunity to get to know his son.

Just the thought of that word had his stomach cramping. He had no idea what to do with a toddler.

He hadn't exactly had a wonderful role model in either of his parents. They'd been too wrapped up in their own worlds to even remember they had children for the most part. His mother and father had been more like Santa Claus or the Easter Bunny, dropping into his life once or twice a year, bringing lots of excitement and presents he didn't really want or need.

Because while they were stingy with their attention, they made damn certain their sons had every material thing they could possibly want.

Too bad those things hadn't made a damn bit of difference to Sawyer. Or Finn, for that matter.

He was not going to be that kind of parent. Refused. He might not know how to handle a baby, but he was going to damn well figure it out.

Genevieve stared at him and he realized he'd been silent a little too long. He needed to get his head in the game before he blew it.

"I don't expect you to forgive me, Genevieve. But I am sorry for what happened. And while you might not believe me—"

"Because you've given me no reason to, but every reason to distrust you."

Finn nodded his head, acknowledging she had a point. Not that he was going to let it stand between him and what he wanted.

"I wasn't stealing the Star that night."

"You were caught with the stone in your possession. And a fake was in its place."

"Genni, I'd had the stone for three days by that point. I came back that night to return it. The plan all along was to take it and disappear. But I couldn't go. For the first time ever, something—someone—was more important to me than the rush of success."

Genevieve stared up at him. A tangle of emotions flitted across her features. God, he loved her terrible poker face.

She was probably one of the most forthright people he'd ever met. And, given the world she'd lived in, that surprised him.

Anyone else might have become jaded or hard, but not Genevieve. She'd been a sweet breath of fresh air. Because he *was* jaded.

She was everything Finn wished he could be and just wasn't.

After several seconds, her tongue licked cautiously across pink lips. "What?"

"I was putting the stone back," he said again.

Getting the Star out had been easy. His plan executed flawlessly.

His conscience had been his downfall. Not to mention his inability to walk away from Genevieve.

He hadn't prepared a plan for returning the stone. Who would have thought that would turn out to be the harder task?

Genevieve frowned. "What's that supposed to change, Finn? You still stole it."

"True, but I couldn't keep it. You were more important."

"If that was true you wouldn't have taken it in the first place."

"If you knew anything about me, you'd realize just how far off that statement really is."

Her mouth flattened into a hard line. "You're right. I know nothing about you. But whose fault is that? I spent weeks thinking I was getting to know this amazing man I was falling in love with only to discover it was all a lie."

"Not all."

"So you've said. But the problem is, there's no way for me to untangle the lies from the truth to figure out what I might be able to trust. And I'm not willing to make the effort even if I could. The past is over, Finn. I'm letting you into my son's life because the court says I don't have a choice. But I fully expect this is a novelty for you. Something your incarceration has convinced you that you should do. In a couple months some other shiny new toy will catch your interest and you'll be gone."

Finn couldn't stop himself. He moved into her personal space, crowding Genevieve in a way that would have had the girl he knew shying away. Instead, she tipped her head back and glared at him.

Pride swelled through his chest, mixing with a healthy dose of amusement. Leaning down, he brought his mouth close enough to feel the heat of her skin caressing his lips and murmured, "Don't count on it. I'm not going anywhere, Genni."

She couldn't hide the shiver that rocked her body. With a huff, Genevieve stepped back, finally putting space between them.

Tilting his head, Finn said, "If we're done dealing with the past—" obviously, they weren't, but they'd at least made a start "—can I please meet Noah now?"

Her glare raked across his body, as if he was lower than the gunk on the bottom of her shoe. She might want to feel that way, but her reaction suggested she didn't really.

Finn simply waited her out, knowing his calm would irritate her. Now he was just being perverse, but he liked the snap of her temper. The way it made her eyes glitter and her skin glow.

Finally, she said, "He's in the back. I'll get him."

She turned to go, no doubt assuming he'd wait. It was the polite thing to do. But he'd never cared about being polite.

Following two steps behind her, he said, "No need. I'll come with you."

Genevieve paused halfway down the darkened hallway. She didn't turn and after several seconds began walking again. It didn't suck that he got a view of her jeans molded to her pert ass. His palm itched to reach out and smack it.

But he wasn't a complete idiot.

They passed by a couple rooms. One was clearly set up as an office. Not just for the boring details no doubt necessary for running her business. Finn also caught glimpses of the tools she used in her work. None of the expensive jewels she sometimes used in her pieces, but shiny bits of rock, mineral and twisted metal.

Another room was most likely a guest room. Genevieve paused in front of a doorway. It was closest to the shut door at the very end of the hallway. Probably her master.

She blocked Finn's view of what was inside, but it really didn't matter. The expression on her face told him everything he needed to know. Pure love and adoration filled her expression.

His own mother had never once looked at him with that kind of love. No one ever had.

No, that wasn't true.

Genevieve had. But she certainly didn't anymore.

She wasn't ready. For Finn or for what was about to happen.

How could she still react to him? After everything the man had done to her...

His betrayal had cut so deep. Starving for affection, approval, acceptance, she'd been ripe to fall for Finn DeLuca's lies. She'd wanted to believe him when he told her she was beautiful. Basked in his praise when he said she was amazingly talented and intelligent.

Considering she'd grown up beneath the harsh and disapproving glare of her grandfather, a man who routinely pointed out that she was useless and couldn't be trusted to do anything correctly, it probably wouldn't have taken much warmth and sunlight for her to flourish. But Finn had given her more than a small taste of what she'd always craved.

Stupid of her for believing him.

But to her credit, she'd been naive and sheltered before. She hadn't been aware of what was lacking in her life until Finn. Hadn't understood that she'd deserved better than the demeaning and degrading verbal and emotional abuse her grandfather had subjected her to.

Now, she was much more aware, and stronger.

Which begged the question, what the hell was wrong with her? Because her body had reacted the moment he walked through her front door. Her heart fluttered and her breath caught. Her palms went clammy and her panties were uncomfortably damp.

Sure, that was understandable considering the man was a walking advertisement for bad-boy perfection. But she *knew* his smile was a facade and every word out of his mouth was suspect.

Apparently, her body was stupid and her brain had a poor memory. At least her heart was less susceptible.

She hoped.

Either way, this visit had absolutely nothing to do with her and Finn. Noah was all that mattered.

Taking a deep, calming breath, Genevieve whispered, "Come meet your son."

Waving him over, she backed from the doorway to give him room. She wanted to train her gaze on Noah, to watch his reaction when he realized there was someone new in the house. But Genevieve couldn't stop her eyes from shifting from the blond-haired boy happily sitting in Maddie's lap to his father.

A tight band constricted her chest at the utter awe stamped across Finn's face. Something unexpected swam through his intent gaze. Something genuine and real. If she didn't know better, Genevieve would have called it longing and hope.

"He looks like my brother."

"He looks like you," Genevieve countered. Except for the blond hair and blue eyes, her son was the spitting image of his father.

Finn gave a quick shake of his head and she wondered if he really couldn't see it. When he was little, it was less obvious, but as Noah had grown, becoming more of a little boy instead of a baby, the resemblance was unavoidable. The only things she'd given their son were his pert nose and bowed mouth. Everything else was pure Finn…including his mischievous, playful nature.

Because, God knew, he hadn't gotten that from Genevieve. But she loved the fact that her son had the opportunity to be a kid. Something she'd never gotten.

Finally sensing them hovering in the doorway, Noah's little head shot up. His expression lit up, as it always did when he saw her. Crossing to them, Genevieve pulled Noah into her arms as she said, "Thanks, Maddie."

"Anytime." Pushing up, Maddie paused on her way out to flash an angry, warning gaze at Finn. Several seconds later the front door reverberated shut, leaving the three of them alone.

Genevieve had the sudden and overwhelming urge to call Maddie back. She needed that buffer, any buffer.

Noah broke the moment, smacking his hands against Genevieve's face and forcing her to look at him. "Mama."

Bouncing him on her hip to resettle him, Genevieve moved closer to Finn. "Noah, this is your daddy. Finn, this is Noah."

Noah tilted his little head sideways, a move she'd seen Finn do not ten minutes before. His cherub lips pursed into a mew and his eyes narrowed. They all held a breath.

That apparently was unnecessary because after several seconds, Noah held his arms out to Finn and demanded, "Up."

To her utter surprise, Finn did just that, scooping her son out of her arms and into his without hesitation. They went nose-to-nose, staring at each other. Noah blinked. And the most gorgeous smile spread across Finn's face.

Pointing to the bookshelf, her son issued a familiar demand. "Book."

Making himself at home, Finn obliged. Grabbing a book from the shelf, he settled into the rocking chair, plopping Noah into his lap like they'd done it a million times.

Genevieve watched for several seconds before quietly turning and leaving.

She couldn't stay. It hurt.

And she hated herself a little because it did.

Casing the place was second nature. Finn didn't even have to try to catalog the security weaknesses as he walked through the front doors at the trendy jewelry boutique in downtown Charleston. The kind of place that catered to wealthy customers even as it proclaimed itself bohemian and unusual.

Hypocritical as far as he was concerned. They wanted to make beaucoup money, but pretend they were in it for the art.

The security guy they'd hired stuck out like a sore thumb, even as he tried to blend in. First, his cheap suit was trying too hard to parade as expensive. Not to mention, the cut of it was terrible, the gun under his arm bulging out visibly when he moved.

Their technology sucked. The cameras were in obvious positions—watching the door, each of the counters and the hallway into the back room. They were at least ten years old and if he had to guess not even digital. No doubt there were blind spots everywhere and the quality of the recordings next to useless.

Sticking his hands in his pockets, Finn wandered slowly through the cramped store. He made a show of inspecting the merchandise, but was really memorizing the staff's movements.

They made it too damn easy.

Knocking over this place would be child's play. With little effort he could have a flawless plan in probably two hours. And most of that time would be replenishing equipment he no longer owned. Hell, he could probably pocket a couple of loose stones without even trying.

But that wasn't why he was here.

Not to mention, he was going straight…for now. Not only did he need to keep on the right side of his parole officer, but no doubt one whiff of theft and Genevieve would deny him access to Noah, court order or not.

"Sir, can I help you?"

Flipping up his wrist, Finn looked at the Piaget there

before flicking his gaze up to the woman who'd finally greeted him. Eight minutes and thirteen seconds. Not great.

"Yes. I'd like to look at some pieces I understand you have on consignment."

The woman visibly perked up. Of course she did. First, he hadn't missed her attention to his watch and the dollar signs she'd finally started ringing up as her gaze swept over him. And all the consignment collections the boutique happened to be hosting were high dollar.

She was about to make a hefty commission.

"Wonderful. What collection were you interested in viewing? We have some wonderful pieces from Maximillian Broussard, a former designer with Harry Winston."

"No, I'm familiar with his work, but his pieces are too heavy for what I'm looking for."

The woman's mouth pursed. Broussard's pieces were no doubt going for more than Genevieve's. For now.

"You're looking for something more delicate and intricate?"

Finn nodded.

"I'm Denise and I have just the thing. Follow me." She spun and trotted off across the store toward what was no doubt a private showroom behind a heavy velvet curtain.

Finn's eyebrows rose as she pulled back the rich sapphire barrier and swept her hand, indicating he should precede her inside. As expected, the room was set up with an elegant table in the center covered in black velvet. There were three chairs and the space was flooded with bright lights. The kind that could catch even the worst cut angle of a gem and make it sparkle like the most flawless diamond.

He accepted a chair and waited. "We have several exclusive pieces from an up-and-coming designer. She's just beginning to make a name for herself, but she's been around gemstones her entire life. She's known for the intricate details of her work and the flawless way she displays stones, emphasizing their strengths and camouflaging their flaws. What kind of piece were you looking for?"

"I'm interested in buying something for a woman who's important to me."

"Necklace, bracelet, earrings…all three?"

He could practically hear the hope in Denise's voice. He was about to make her ever-loving day. "Possibly. If I find the right pieces. Why don't you show me what you have and we'll go from there?"

Denise nearly clapped her hands together with glee. "Absolutely. Let me pour you a drink while I go gather a few things to show you. Bourbon? Wine?"

"Bourbon would be lovely." He really didn't want it, but it always set people at ease when they left you something to do with your hands and mouth.

The minute Denise was gone, Finn abandoned the uncomfortable chair and began wandering the room. If he'd wanted to, he could have been into the back rooms, probably cracked their shitty safe and had a pocket stuffed full of stones before she returned.

His palms itched and the enticing memory of adrenaline and triumph called to him. Stupid people practically begged to be taken advantage of. He had no respect for those who refused to protect what they valued. However, this place hardly presented a big enough challenge to honestly tempt him. It wasn't worth it.

Denise bustled back in and spread several trays out across the top of the table. Finn would have known the pieces were Genevieve's even if there hadn't been a discreet card with her name in a filigreed logo tucked into the corner of each.

They were so her. Light and gorgeous. Breathtaking and delicate. But with a core of strength emanating from the twisting, looping metal surrounding the beautiful stones. None of the pieces held diamonds, which didn't necessarily surprise him. That would have been too expected.

Besides, Genevieve liked color.

One grouping had the dark, deep red of Burmese rubies. Another with sapphires and water opals. They were all gorgeous. But the last set of emeralds called to him. Maybe because the varying shades of green reminded him of Genevieve's eyes. The paler green center with the evergreen ring at the edge.

Pulling the tray closer, Finn let his gaze travel across the matching set. The necklace was gorgeous, a single teardrop emerald with exquisite saturation and color. Finn itched to ask for a loupe, but didn't want to reveal the extent of his knowledge. The stone was small, but he'd guess almost inclusion free. No doubt it had cost Genevieve quite a bit.

The stones in the matching bracelet and earrings were smaller and less impressive, but that wasn't surprising. The necklace was the showpiece. He could imagine it nestled right in the hollow of Genevieve's throat.

"I'll take them," he declared, pushing the tray away and sitting back. The spindly chair creaked ominously beneath him. Seriously, this place needed a full upgrade on everything.

"Wonderful. She's a lucky woman."

Finn fought back a laugh. That might be, but something told him if—no, when—Genevieve found out he'd purchased these pieces she was going to be less than pleased.

There was more than one way to get his money into her hands.

Three

"You sold the three emerald pieces."

Genevieve's belly clenched. She should be so happy. That sale alone would support her and Noah for the next several months. And if any of the other sets had sold she wouldn't be conflicted. But from the moment she'd held that teardrop emerald she'd felt a connection to it.

It wasn't the first time. And hopefully, it wouldn't be the last. She always felt a kinship with the stones she worked with. She routinely spent days or weeks studying them. Analyzing them from every angle to determine the best way to put them on display.

But there'd been something very special about that emerald.

However, she couldn't afford to keep a stone simply because she wanted to. She'd had almost fifty grand

tied up in that emerald alone. That was one of the draw-
backs of running her own design company. The materials she worked with were expensive. But they paid off
when they sold.

She hadn't sold a piece in a few weeks so this really came at a great time. That's what she was going to
focus on. Maybe after the collection launch she'd think
about planning a trip for Noah to Disney next year. For
his birthday.

"Genevieve? Did you hear me?"

Shaking her head, she brought her focus back to Eric,
the owner of one of the boutiques she'd consigned with.
"Yes, I'm sorry. That's wonderful! Can you tell me who
bought the pieces?"

She always liked to know something about the people
who purchased her jewelry. It helped her complete the
circle in her head. To imagine the look of excitement,
or shock and surprise, on a woman's face when her hus-
band presented her with one of her pieces. She liked
to know if there was a story behind it. Was it to com-
memorate the birth of a child? Or fifty years together?

It gave her a sense of pride and happiness to know
something she created could give those feelings to
someone else.

"I don't know much. Denise didn't get a lot of details. A gentleman came in, but he wasn't certain what
he wanted. He chose the emerald pieces as soon as she
brought them out, though."

Well, that was something. Maybe the person who'd
purchased them had connected to them as much as she
had. That gave her a little bit of comfort.

"Can you send over the name and address?"

She liked to send her customers a personal note of thanks. It was something she'd done in the beginning and many of her customers had made repeat purchases, partly because they liked her style, but also because they appreciated the personal touch.

It was one of the few downsides to expanding her business. She wasn't certain how she would maintain that same connection.

The upcoming collection had the potential to make a huge splash. Her partnership with Mitchell Brothers Jewelry, a major chain within the southeast, was already receiving some amazing press. It was nice to have that kind of experience and marketing behind her collection.

In a matter of weeks, she would go from having her pieces displayed in a handful of boutiques to appearing in over fifty locations in twelve states across the South.

It would mean more security for Noah. She'd simply have to find a way to keep the personal touch she'd become known for.

"Absolutely," Eric said. "I'll email the information to you. And we'll send the direct deposit within the week."

"Thanks, Eric. I appreciate it."

Genevieve hung up and walked back into the studio where she designed. Noah was with Nicole, the woman Genevieve had hired to watch her son while she worked. Nicole was a college student, which was convenient for Genevieve, who often worked weird hours when she was in the middle of a design. She had at least another two hours before she needed to be home.

She stared at the stones spread across the table before

her. They were gorgeous. A perfect example of alexandrite, a rare semiprecious stone known for color shifting based on the light. She'd been studying the seven stones for the past few days, trying to decide what they were destined to be.

The biggest was slightly over a carat. Three more were roughly three quarters each. The other three varied, but were all just below a half. It would make sense to set the largest stone in a necklace, two of the smaller as stud earrings and then a bracelet of some kind.

That would be logical. But that wasn't what her instincts were calling for her to do. The problem was, no alternative was coming to her, either.

She let her fingers sift across the stones, enjoying their cool surface and the way they rolled beneath her touch. She could feel the hard edges. See the brilliant fire trapped deep inside.

Scooping them into her palm, she rearranged them once more, hoping inspiration would hit.

Nothing.

She'd sunk a lot of money into these stones and really needed to finish it before the opening. Frustration tightened her shoulders until they pulled up close to her ears.

The ding of an email arriving on her phone cut through the unhappy silence of her studio.

Perfect. She needed a distraction.

Snatching up her phone, Genevieve unlocked the screen and pulled up the email from Eric.

A growl escaped when she read the information he'd forwarded.

She was going to kill Finn.

* * *

Finn was naked when the doorman buzzed up to let him know he had a visitor—a female—waiting for him downstairs. The only woman who had his address was Stone's girlfriend, Piper. And he couldn't think of a single reason she'd stop by. Especially without calling.

A half smile twisted his lips. That just left Genevieve.

The familiar edge of excitement shot through his veins. Whatever brought her to his doorstep at seven at night, it wasn't likely to be because she wanted to rip his clothes off.

Grabbing a pair of sweatpants, Finn slipped them on, but didn't bother with a shirt. Padding across his penthouse loft, he rubbed a towel across his wet hair as he went. Pulling open his front door, he left it wide-open and wandered back into his living room.

No doubt she'd find him.

It didn't take her long. He heard the sharp tap of her feet against his floor. She was wearing heels. He loved when she wore heels. They made her calves and thighs look amazing.

His front door slammed shut and her voice hissed behind him, "How many times do I have to say this? I don't want your money."

Finished with the towel, Finn tossed it onto the arm of the sofa before taking his time to turn. His gaze traveled slowly down her body. It wasn't intentional. He simply couldn't stop his response to her.

She was even more gorgeous when she was pissed.

Her green eyes spit fire and twin flags of color stained

her cheeks. Her hands were balled into fists and set high and tight on her hips. Her entire body leaned toward him even as she maintained about ten feet of distance.

"You've made that clear."

"And yet, that didn't stop you from pulling a stunt."

"Stunt?" Finn decided to play dumb, although it probably wasn't going to get him anywhere. But he'd learned a long time ago not to admit guilt unless he knew for certain he was already caught. "What are you talking about?"

"Oh, don't feign stupid. We both know you're not. You're always five steps ahead of everyone around you."

"Thank you?" he asked, pretty certain she hadn't meant her words to be the compliment they were.

"Return the pieces."

Finn shrugged. "No."

"You don't want them or need them. And I refuse to take your guilt money. Noah and I don't need it."

He'd been in a perfectly jovial mood until that moment. Dropping the affable facade, Finn quickly closed the gap between them. Genevieve apparently realized her tactical error because she scrambled several steps backward. However, she'd miscalculated because that move brought her up hard against the exposed brick wall.

He heard her body hit with a thud, but he didn't stop until both his hands were spread on either side of her head. The rough brick edges scraped across his palms. His thigh brushed against hers. And he tried not to notice the way her breath stuttered in her lungs.

"Let's make one thing crystal clear, Genevieve. Guilt

has nothing to do with anything I'm doing. You're raising my son and there's no reason for either you or he to go without."

"I'm perfectly capable of providing for *my* son, Finn."

"Yes, I'm aware. I've seen your tax returns for the last three years and have a detailed financial report for your business. I know exactly how much money you have tied up in materials and inventory. I know you're stretched thin preparing for this opening, but we both know you'll be fine once that happens because you're a brilliant designer. The world just doesn't know it yet."

Genevieve blinked. Her mouth thinned with irritation, but he didn't pause long enough to give her a chance to voice it.

"However, there's no need for you ever to be in a position to worry. I have enough money to support a third-world country."

"Then by all means, give *them* a check for a million dollars."

"I have."

She tilted her head sideways, a tell indicating he'd just surprised her. Which shouldn't surprise him, but it did. It also hurt a little. He wasn't a heartless monster, dammit.

"You wouldn't accept my help any other way, so I found a way you couldn't refuse."

"I won't let you purchase those pieces."

"Genevieve," he murmured, disappointment filling his voice. "We both know I'm already in possession of the emeralds."

"Then give them back."

"No. They're mine."

"What are you going to do with them?"

"None of your business."

Her teeth ground together, frustration and something more personal filling her gaze.

"I'll simply refuse the money from Eric."

Finn used his height advantage to crowd even farther into her personal space. Genevieve shifted, but there was nowhere for her to go so the gesture simply had her body brushing tantalizingly against his.

Every cell in his body lit up. The driving need to touch her, taste her, take her was a pounding tattoo deep in his blood. Instead, he gently cupped his hand beneath her jaw and brought her gaze to meet his.

"Don't do that," he said. His words might have been soft; however, the order beneath them was anything but.

"Or what?" she challenged, eyes flashing fire.

Her mouth was so close he could feel the heat of her breath against his skin. Her lips, parted in anger, practically begged him to touch.

A temptation Finn couldn't deny. His fingers slipped across the silky texture of her cheek. It had been so long since he'd touched her. Too long.

And this moment wasn't nearly enough. Not when memories of Genevieve, writhing beneath him in pleasure, filled his brain.

His grip on her tightened. Finn pulled her mouth to his, the driving need to steal a taste of her too much to ignore.

The moment his lips touched hers it was all over. Heat and need claimed him. The emptiness he'd been carrying around for so long began to ache. That throb only she'd ever been able to touch.

Any good intentions he might have been able to scrounge up burned to ash. And he simply began to take. Opening his mouth, Finn released a sigh of relief when she did the same, unconsciously letting him in. Her hands gripped his shoulders, not pulling him closer, but not pushing him away.

He took everything she was willing to give him. Darting his tongue deep inside her mouth, relishing the sweet, spicy taste of her suffusing his senses.

Nope, he needed to get a grip.

Pulling away, Finn dropped his forehead to hers. He simply froze, trying to find his equilibrium…and sense. His harsh breaths mingled with her stuttered pulls of air.

Eventually, he put a little space between them. Just enough to be able to look her straight in the eye and say, "I don't want to take anything from you, Genevieve. I promise. I just want to give. Please, let me."

Shit, shit, shit.
She was an idiot.

Because she wanted to believe him. But her brain was screaming at her that she shouldn't. She knew better. He'd fooled her once with his earnest expression and slick words.

But he also wasn't wrong.

She really needed the money from the sale of the emeralds. She'd been eyeing some black opals that would make an amazing choker, but she just didn't have the capital to invest in the stones right now.

There was a part of her that hated knowing Finn was going to be the one to own the emeralds, as well. And she refused to let herself contemplate him giving them to another woman. The expression of joy and surprise on that woman's face as he leaned close to clasp the necklace around her slim neck…

Nope, Genevieve wasn't going there.

Besides, her commission from the sale wasn't anywhere near what he'd tried to give her a couple months ago. That check had smelled of guilt and she wasn't ready to let him off the hook by accepting it.

This, however, was a business exchange. Nothing more and nothing less.

"Fine. Keep the emeralds. I'll take the commission. As long as you promise not to buy any more pieces."

Finn shrugged. "I promise not to buy any pieces for the sole purpose of giving you money, how about that?"

She couldn't contemplate any other reason for him to invest hundreds of thousands of dollars in jewelry right now, so… "Fine. Thank you. There are some black opals I've been coveting. I'll be able to buy them and finish the last two pieces for my collection."

"Mmm," he murmured. "Black opals?"

Genevieve felt the excitement bubbling up inside her and couldn't tamp it down. "They're gorgeous. The play-of-color is…unbelievable, and they're perfect for a choker I've designed but just haven't found the right stones for. The shades of blue and purple against the black background...and they all came from the same rough stone. They're just..."

She hadn't realized how gushy she sounded until she looked up to find Finn staring at her. Slowly, the excitement leaked out. Genevieve literally felt her entire body deflating.

"I'm sorry. You probably don't care."

"Don't," he said, stepping closer. "I enjoy seeing the fire in your eyes while you talk about stones. Your passion for what you do is one of the things I like most about you, Genevieve, and always have."

She shook her head, unsure how to handle what he'd said. What was she supposed to do with that?

Sure, she missed having someone to share her enthusiasm with. That was one of the things she missed most about working at Reilly. She'd been surrounded by people who understood her stupid obsession with hard bits of minerals and rock.

It was something she and Finn had shared before. For those few weeks he'd been a part of her life, she'd had a confidant who wanted to have a conversation about gemstones.

Of course, that was because he'd been trying to pull information from her so he could steal her family's most prized possession.

Shifting away from him, Genevieve waved her hand. "It doesn't matter. I hope whomever you bought the emeralds for enjoys them. Those pieces had a special place in my heart."

Finn tipped his head sideways and his gaze narrowed. "I'm hopeful their new owner will appreciate having them."

Something sharp pinched in the center of her chest. "No doubt."

Crap.

"Well… I should leave." Genevieve waved lamely toward the door she'd burst through only a few minutes ago. Where was the ball of anger that had fueled her then?

Incinerated by that kiss.

That stupid kiss that she was just going to pretend never happened.

Finn watched as she backed slowly toward the door. The way his gaze followed her, the corner of his lips tipped into a telling half smile, made her itchy and uncomfortable. He had the uncanny ability to make her feel unfettered and awkward at the same time. Like he saw something deep inside her that she wasn't sure really existed.

Pausing with her hand on the knob, Genevieve fought against the weird desire to lock the door and stay on this side instead of walking away. "Call me later in the week and you can stop by to see Noah again."

There was nothing suppressed about the smile that brightened Finn's face. "I'd like that."

A few days ago, she'd been worried about Finn's ability to be a dad. But after watching him with her son yesterday, she was no longer concerned. Finn was a natural with Noah, possibly because in many ways Finn still acted like a child himself.

Although that didn't precisely assuage all of her concerns. In fact, it only added a couple more.

Closing the door behind her, Genevieve found herself sagging against it, unable to walk away. Her knees were mushy and her legs next to useless.

And she was no longer confident in her ability to be in the same room with Finn DeLuca and not want him.

Four

Twenty-four hours later, Finn couldn't get that kiss out of his head. Passion had never been their issue. In fact, from the moment he laid eyes on Genevieve, he'd wanted her.

Which had ultimately been his downfall.

At first, he'd been drawn to her in the same way he'd fallen in love with a Rembrandt when he was a teenager or a glorious ruby the size of his fist ten years later. Incidentally, he'd eventually owned both.

He'd always had an affinity for beautiful things. And there was certainly something ethereal and wholesome about Genevieve. So different from the jaded world Finn had lived in for his entire life.

Early on, he'd convinced himself it was an act. It had to be. No one was that naive and trusting. Especially knowing her grandfather, Lackland Reilly, and his influence on her life. But Finn soon realized she *was* that trusting.

Or she used to be.

He'd ruined that about her, and right now he hated himself for stealing the clear innocence that had shone from her eyes. He might have replaced the Star, but he couldn't fix the other damage he'd caused.

Although watching her with their son…he might even be more attracted to her now than he'd been before.

Lackland had worked hard to keep Genevieve sheltered and unaware of how the world really worked. He'd homeschooled her, surrounded her with nothing but adults who did and said what he demanded. And he'd expected the same of Genevieve, to follow his commands without question. Treating her more like an employee than a family member. A commodity.

And that had pissed Finn off. It wasn't the first time he'd encountered that kind of dictatorial sense of entitlement in their world. And hell, he'd never given a damn about how anyone else was treated.

Until Genevieve.

He'd always sensed an inner strength, hidden deep. Like the roughest uncut diamond, just waiting for the skill and patience to bring out the sparkle and fire.

Why did it bother him that he hadn't been the catalyst that had brought her fire forth?

Although maybe he could take some of the credit. The way she'd stormed into his apartment yesterday, her eyes blazing, ready to go toe-to-toe with him…

The Genevieve he'd known before wouldn't have had the backbone to do that.

Even now, Finn felt his sex stir at the memory. He'd been unable to control his reaction to her. His physical need to touch and taste, to capture that energy and make it his own.

But he couldn't give in to that need. Not without jeopardizing what he really wanted. Getting distracted by Genevieve had cost him before…he wasn't willing to make that mistake again. Their attraction was dangerous. It made him sloppy and stupid.

What really mattered was that she'd said he could visit Noah again. A step in the right direction, but he wanted more. He wanted to be able to show his son the world.

Finn needed to move slowly with Genevieve. Convince her that he was different from the man who'd seduced her for his own purposes three years ago. Because he was.

Or he wanted to be. For his son. For the family he'd never thought he'd have again when Sawyer died.

The phone on the table in front of him buzzed, rattling against the wooden surface. Scooping it up, he punched the green button to answer.

"Stone."

"I've got the equipment you asked for. Please tell me you're not doing anything illegal with it. No, wait. On second thought, don't tell me a damn thing. Deniability is a beautiful thing."

Finn laughed. One good thing about Stone, he always managed to make Finn smile.

"I'm not doing anything illegal." Exactly... Although perhaps he was walking a fine line. Genevieve probably wouldn't agree to the surveillance equipment he was about to install outside her studio and home, but that was only because she didn't understand how vulnerable she really was.

He, on the other hand, knew exactly where her security weaknesses were hiding. And he intended to patch a few of the holes...until he could convince her to give him access inside to cover the rest. No way was he going to let something—someone—important to him remain needlessly vulnerable. He robbed idiots like that and he refused to be an idiot.

On this, he'd risk asking for forgiveness instead of permission. Genevieve and Noah were important to him. Her business and designs were important to her. So he was going to protect them.

"Uh-huh," Stone's skeptical voice ghosted down the line. "You've got enough cameras, microphones and storage capacity here to make the Met envious."

"That's a nasty exaggeration."

"Fine, just tell me you're not going to do something stupid."

"I'm going to set up external surveillance at Genevieve's studio and home. Her security leaves a lot to be desired."

The silence that followed practically screamed Stone's disapproval. His friend was fully aware of the history between Finn and Genevieve. He was also privy to the six-month fight Finn had just engaged in to get access to his son.

No doubt Stone thought this was asking for trouble. And maybe he was right, but Finn was going to do it, anyway.

Finally, Stone said, "I'm going out on a limb here and guessing she has no idea her every move is about to be recorded?"

"Uh…" Finn really didn't want to answer that question.

"Jesus," Stone swore. "You're gonna end up back in jail, aren't you?"

"No." Finn had no intention of getting caught, either with this, or with anything else. "Can your team install everything? And set up the feed on my computer and phone?"

Stone sighed. "Yeah. I'll send someone over tomorrow. Let them know how you want it all set up. It should only take a couple hours."

"They'll be discreet?"

"You mean, they won't tip your baby mama off that she's being watched?"

Finn had to bite back a retort at Stone's words. He knew the man had used them on purpose, hoping to get a rise out of Finn.

"Yes," he ground out.

"They're skilled at being unseen when I need them to be."

Perfect.

Genevieve stared at the jewels sparkling on the table in front of her. They were gorgeous. Something about them made her chest tighten with joy and anticipation.

Her blood thrummed faster in her veins, sort of like it did the minute Finn got close enough for her to smell his spicy, tempting scent. Whatever shampoo or soap he used, she wanted to have it banned in all fifty states... as a lethal weapon.

Nope, she wasn't going to think about him right now. She'd spent the last couple days trying to wipe out the memory of her tirade at his apartment...and the kiss that had sent her scurrying for safety.

Because she was a damn fool. And her body epitomized the definition of weakness.

Even knowing exactly the kind of man he was and the deception he was capable of...she'd wanted him. So much. Where had her libido been the last three years? Because it certainly had been MIA.

Even now, the damn man was messing with her life. She'd come into the studio to work. She really needed to get this piece finished...which was a problem since she couldn't even seem to get it started.

She'd been staring at the stones, moving them around on the table, as her mind ping-ponged ninety miles an hour on everything except her work. No, that wasn't true. She knew exactly what her mind had been focused on.

Flipping her cell phone over, she glanced at the screen and registered that it was close to midnight. She needed to head out and let Nicole go home. She didn't have class in the morning, but that didn't mean she wasn't looking forward to crawling into her own bed.

Frustrated that she'd wasted several hours and accomplished nothing, Genevieve gathered the stones and locked them back into the state-of-the art vault where she kept her loose stones and finished pieces.

That was one thing Nick, her only employee and head of security, had insisted on. He'd allowed her to scrimp in other areas in exchange for an expensive-as-hell vault. His rationale was that anyone just knocking over the place would be outclassed and leave empty-handed. She'd been around the business long enough to understand the value of protecting the investment she'd made in materials.

But at the end of the day, even if this was her liveli-hood, the gemstones were just things. Certainly, they were beautiful, but so was the sound of her son's laugh-ter. At least to her.

Locking the back door, Genevieve took several steps outside when an unexpected shiver snaked down her spine. The hair on the back of her neck stood on end and she paused midstride. A burst of adrenaline shot into her system.

But she had no idea why.

Gaze darting around the empty parking lot, Gene-vieve attempted to find something out of place. But ev-erything was quiet and still. Shadows shifted, but they were leaves from the grand oak trees at the back of the property rustling in the late-night breeze.

It was her imagination. She was being paranoid, that was all. Quickening her pace, Genevieve grasped her keys, unlocked the door to her SUV, slid inside and quickly locked it again.

Her heart was beating way too fast considering nothing had happened. Shaking her head, Genevieve cranked her car and headed home. She needed sleep, that was all.

She'd take another crack at the alexandrite tomorrow. Maybe during the day. A change of scenery might be what she needed. In the meantime, she was going to head home and spend some time with her sketch pad. Maybe brilliance would strike.

Finn stared at the computer screen open in front of him. His loft was pitch-black, the only light coming from the glow in front of him. His feet were kicked up onto the coffee table, a glass of red wine close to his elbow.

Anyone who walked in would probably assume he was completely relaxed, watching a movie or something.

In reality, he was desperately trying to control his temper.

It was his turn to want to race across town, barge into Genevieve's home and read her the riot act. What was she thinking, working alone that late at night? The neighborhood her studio was in was decent, but any place could be dangerous after midnight.

Especially when you added the temptation of pricey gemstones.

And from what he'd gathered, her late-night foray to the studio wasn't an anomaly. She hadn't even bothered to call in the yahoo she'd hired to handle her security.

Oh, you better believe he'd had the idiot checked. And while on the outside he appeared capable of handling the job, it was obvious he wasn't. Or Genevieve never would have been at the studio alone at midnight.

Clearly, he'd gotten the job because she'd known him from her time at Reilly. And, from watching the man for the last few days, Finn did not like the way his gaze followed Genevieve. Finn's gut told him more than loyalty had what's-his-name following Genni when she left the family business.

Finn sat up straighter in his chair when Genevieve's car appeared on the right half of the split screen. Maybe he needed to ask Stone to put a tracker on her car so he could monitor her on the way home. Although that was probably crossing a line, the dead space between her leaving the studio and arriving at her place made him nervous.

Genevieve parked in her driveway, pulling in beside the old sedan her babysitter drove. She disappeared inside only to reappear on the front stoop as the other woman left.

Nicole's hair was pulled up into a knot on the top of her head, but at some point it had gotten a little off-kilter. Her eyes were heavy-lidded and she moved sluggishly, as if she was half-asleep.

In contrast, Genevieve was wide-awake.

She gave the other woman a hug, asked her a question, which was answered with a definitive nod, and then watched as she drove away. Crossing her arms over her chest, Genevieve stood outside for several seconds before slipping back inside.

Finn watched the progression of lights as they went dark throughout her house. He had no doubt she stood at

Noah's doorway for several seconds before disappearing into her own room. Not only because there was a pause before the hallway light was extinguished, but because that was the kind of mother she would be.

It took about fifteen minutes for all the lights in her home to flip off. He should follow suit and go to bed, as well, but he couldn't. Not merely because of his irritation at Genevieve's lack of self-preservation.

He wanted to be there with her, slipping into bed beside her. Yes, touching and tasting her, but also pulling her close and tucking her into the shelter of his body. Falling asleep to the quiet sound of her breathing. The heat of her skin sinking deep into his own.

Genevieve made him want things he shouldn't.

Nope, he wasn't going there.

Finn was about to close the lid of his laptop when something made him pause. His hand rested on the top of the lid as his gaze sharpened on the left side of his screen.

Right there. Again. A flicker.

His heart kicked inside his chest, ticking into a faster rhythm, one that was comfortable and familiar. He lived for the heightened physical state, that hit adrenaline gave during high-stress situations.

Something wasn't right.

Pulling the feed at Genevieve's studio up full screen, Finn zoomed in tighter and waited.

It didn't take long for one of the many shadows to move against all the others, materializing into a dark figure skulking at the back door.

Shit.

Before he could react, Finn watched it open wide enough for whoever was there to slip inside.

Vaulting up from his position on the sofa, Finn juggled the computer in one hand while he snatched up his phone with the other. The first call he made was to the police. The second was to Stone.

The third was to Genevieve.

Genevieve tossed and turned for about twenty minutes, her brain simply refusing to settle. Finally, in that space right before falling asleep, her body had just begun to sink down into the bed when her cell phone rang out from the bedside table.

The noise startled her, jolting her upright. Her brain was sluggish enough that it took her a couple seconds before registering what the sound was. Snatching up the phone for fear the noise would wake Noah, she didn't recognize the number before hitting Accept. Telemarketers didn't call after midnight, so it really didn't matter. But if this was a wrong number she was going to get cranky.

"Hello," she whispered, resituating herself in bed so she could rest against the headboard.

"Genevieve?"

Her eyebrows beetled. "Finn?"

"Yeah, listen—"

She cut him off. "What the hell are you doing calling me this late? Whatever you have to say can wait until in the morning."

"Genevieve." Finn's voice was urgent and demanding, much different from the unconcerned billionaire she knew. "Someone broke into your studio. I've called the police and a friend, but you should get over here."

Blinking, she didn't even know how to respond to what he'd just said. "What?" was about all her brain would spit out.

"I'm so sorry to call this way," he responded, his voice going soft and apologetic.

Her grandfather's snide voice sounded in the back of her mind. *Use your head, girl. It isn't a coincidence this is happening just days after he's back in your life.*

She hadn't spoken to her grandfather in three years. She'd avoided any chance encounter by cutting ties with anyone in his life. And it pissed her off that even now his voice could invade her mind. Influence her thoughts.

But, dammit, he wasn't wrong.

"Is this your fault?"

"What? No. Why would you even ask that?"

Why wouldn't she? He was guilty of breaking into her grandfather's vault...and most likely a hundred more. Although she couldn't for the life of her figure out his angle for calling and telling her.

But that didn't mean he didn't have one.

"The police are on their way," he reiterated.

For some reason, that statement made her stomach dive straight to her toes. He was serious if he'd called the cops. She couldn't fathom Finn DeLuca voluntarily communicating with the authorities.

Dammit.

"I'll be there in ten minutes." Genevieve didn't bother waiting for Finn's response before hanging up.

Vaulting out of bed, she raced to Noah's room and

gently scooped him up, blanket and all. He barely stirred when she strapped him into his car seat, mumbling a couple nonsense words before his half-opened eyelids closed again.

The streets were deserted as she raced across the city to her studio. Several stoplights caught her, red only to make her impatiently wait while terrible thoughts spun through her brain.

Her show was ruined. Every single one of her pieces was inside the safe in her studio. She was an idiot for leaving them all there, but considering she had nowhere else to secure them...it had been her only choice.

Turning the corner, Genevieve wanted to scream and cry when she saw the trio of police cars parked haphazardly in the street outside her studio. Blue-and-red lights flashed across the empty pavement, bouncing off the brick facade of the buildings surrounding them. The revolving lights made her dizzy.

She had no idea why she bothered to park inside the lines of the space in front of the sidewalk, other than habit.

Genevieve was half out of the car when a figure appeared inside her opened door. She yelped before realizing who was standing beside her.

Finn's hand cupped her elbow, supporting her as she stood. A zing of electricity shot up her arm and across her chest.

She couldn't deal with him right now.

Shaking him off, Genevieve maneuvered away, rounding the back of the car to the other side.

"I don't need this right now, Finn. Please go away."

Without waiting for his response, she opened the back door and ducked inside so she could gently extricate Noah, hoping the whole time that he might remain asleep. Although that probably wouldn't last long.

She had the buckle undone and the straps off his arms when she felt Finn's heat at her back.

Seriously, she just couldn't right now.

But before she could say anything, his hands were over hers, stopping her from finishing what she was doing.

Strong hands grasped her and hauled her backward out of the open doorway.

That's when he made a huge tactical error. Finn positioned himself between her and her son.

"What the hell are you doing?" she angrily whispered. "Get out of the way. This is not the time."

"No."

"Excuse me?"

"I won't let you wake him up. Noah should be home, asleep in his own bed right now."

"No joke, asshole. And the sooner you get out of my way, the sooner I can speak to the police, figure out what the hell is going on here, just how much damage has been done, so I can go home and put Noah back to bed."

"Why didn't you call Nicole back?"

Had he really just asked her that? "Because it's almost one o'clock in the morning."

"Maddie, then."

"Because that would make it better? I'm not calling anyone in the middle of the night to take care of my son. I'm perfectly capable. I'm not happy about his sleep being disturbed, but it's not an everyday occurrence. Shit happens, and as a single mother, I do the best I can to handle the obstacles." Her voice began to escalate, until it was loud enough to echo off the walls beside them. "I'm damn good at it, because I've been doing it for a long time. Noah and I can handle this. We don't need you here."

His entire face pulled tight, aristocratic features sharp and pinched. His dark coffee eyes flashed with an unexpected fire that had breath backing into her lungs.

"Tough. I'm here, anyway. I'm not judging your decisions as a mother, Genevieve. You're a damn good one and I didn't need the report sitting on my desk to tell me that. I never doubted you'd be anything but a good mother. You have an uncanny ability to put everyone else's needs before your own, a trait that motherhood has only enhanced. You need to go inside, speak to the police and tell them what's missing. I can't do that for you. What I can do is take our son home and put him back to bed. Because there's no reason he has to be here."

Genevieve stared at Finn for several seconds. A lump formed in her throat, but she refused to let it build into the emotional breakdown that threatened.

Was she an idiot for contemplating letting him take Noah?

Probably. Finn DeLuca was selfish, egotistical and too charming for his own good. But there wasn't a single part of her afraid he wouldn't take care of their son.

The man had fought too hard to get access to Noah to screw it up by doing something stupid.

"You don't know anything about taking care of a toddler."

"True, but I think I can handle unhooking the harness and getting him back into bed. Unless you expect he's going to wake up and want to throw a rave?"

Unexpected laughter burst out of her. She could totally see Finn throwing a toddler techno party, complete with funneling chocolate milk and popping fruit snacks like they were pills.

She was clearly exhausted and punch-drunk.

Her gaze drifted behind Finn to where Noah sat in his car seat. His little head was lolling against the headrest, completely oblivious to the blue-and-red lights flashing intermittently across his face.

She didn't want him here.

"Fine," she found herself saying before the decision had even fully formed. "The gold one is the key to the door from the garage." Grabbing his hand, she slapped her keys into Finn's palm.

Before she could pull away, his fingers closed around her wrist, trapping her in place. Digging something out of his pocket, he gently uncurled her fingers before placing a single car key in her palm. Instinctively, her hand closed around the hard plastic, still warm from his body heat.

"I parked by the back door. I'll text you when we get home and he's back in bed."

Nodding, Genevieve took a huge step back. "Thanks."

Her mind was a jumbled mess as she watched Finn

fold his tall, muscular body into her small SUV and back away. She stared at his brake lights until they disappeared around the corner.

And only when an officer walked up beside her saying, "Ms. Reilly? I need to ask you a few questions," did she shake herself back into focus on what was going on around her.

Five

It didn't take Genevieve long to realize nothing had been stolen. Thank God whoever had broken in hadn't gotten to the vault. Probably because Finn had called in the cavalry.

It really sucked that she was annoyed and grateful at the same time, but the man had the uncanny ability to stir up a jumbled mess of emotions inside her.

A back window had been shattered. Tiny shards of glass twinkled in the bright lights someone had flipped on overhead. They reminded her of the jewels the thief had no doubt planned to snag.

Her design table had been knocked over, a spool of thin copper wire unraveling as it rolled across the floor. Papers from the desk were strewn across the room as if someone had gathered them up and just tossed them into the air. Invoices, design sketches, consignment contracts…everywhere.

But on the far wall, the vault stood, untouched.

Everything was a mess, but that could be remedied.

"I'm sorry." Nick, her head of security—her only security—walked up beside her. He shook his head as he surveyed the destruction littering the floor.

"For what? You didn't do this."

He hummed in the back of his throat. "It's my job to prevent stuff like this. We're just lucky someone saw what was happening and called it in."

Weren't they just. And as soon as she got home she was going to have a nice chat with the Good Samaritan to figure out just why the hell he'd been watching her studio late at night.

Not to mention how he'd known her babysitter's name and that Genevieve would be calling her *back*. Which implied he already knew she'd been there and left once tonight.

Maybe he was pissed someone had beaten him to breaking in. Because, really, the only reason she could think he'd be so aware of the activity at her studio would be for casing the place.

But she wasn't about to bring that up to Nick. Not yet, anyway.

"Luckily, none of the pieces were taken. It'll probably take me a couple days to clean up and organize, which will put me behind on the last two pieces. But I'll figure out how to make it work."

Assuming she ever figured out what she wanted to do with those damn stones. If she didn't…a break-in wasn't the only thing that could tank her career before it ever really got off the ground.

"I'll review the surveillance footage, see if I can find anything that might help us catch this guy. Identify any weaknesses we can shore up quickly and easily."

"And cheaply," Genevieve added with an unhappy twist of her lips.

Nick nodded, his own mouth pulling tight.

"I'm pretty sure this was just a smash and grab. The back window was an easy target, which I already knew. I'll figure out why the glass break malfunctioned. We should have gotten an alert the minute that window shattered."

"Thanks, Nick," Genevieve said, exhaustion stealing through her body.

She'd already spent over an hour answering questions about her movements that evening, helping the police piece together a timeline. She couldn't even think about starting to tackle the mess, although at the very least the window needed to be taken care of.

On a sigh, she walked forward, ignoring the crunch of glass beneath her feet.

"If you'll wait for a few more minutes, I'll find a board to nail up over the window and drive you home."

"Thanks. I'm fine to drive home. But I'd really appreciate if you'd handle the window. I just don't have the energy. I was here late working and had just started to fall asleep when I got the call."

Nick didn't look happy but he didn't argue with her, which was a good thing because she couldn't have handled that right now. "Did you call in Nicole?"

"No."

Nick's eyes narrowed. "Then who's with Noah?"

She sighed. This wasn't going to go over well. Nick had been her friend when she worked at Reilly and was fully aware of the events surrounding her pregnancy… and the last six months as she'd fought to keep Finn out of her son's life.

"His dad."

Shock crossed Nick's face, quickly replaced with an anger that flushed his skin a mottled red. "What? How the hell did that happen?"

Not that she needed to explain herself to Nick, but she felt a responsibility to do it, anyway. He'd stuck by her side, following her even before she'd had enough money to offer him a job. He was a good friend, if a little overly protective at times. Although that was sorta his job.

"It's a long story. Let's just say he was in the right place at the right time when I needed him."

Nick's entire face twisted into a sneer. "Of course he was. Hell, he's probably responsible for the break-in in the first place. Did you think about that?"

"Yes. But it doesn't make sense. He bought the emeralds the other day. Because I refused to take his money for Noah and he was hell-bent on getting some funds in my hands. Why would he do that only to turn around and rob me?"

Nick shook his head. "You can be so naive. I have to admit it's one of the things I like best about you… normally. But not tonight. Who says his goal was stealing from you? Let me guess, he was the one who called the police."

"Yes."

"Playing the white knight is exactly the kind of con he'd set up simply to get in your good graces and earn your trust."

Nick wasn't wrong. Finn was definitely capable of orchestrating complex scenarios in order to accomplish whatever goal he wanted.

And he *had* made it clear he was hoping to become a part of her and Noah's life, whether she wanted him there or not.

"I'm not naive, Nick. I haven't been for three years."

Finn was responsible for that, and not entirely because he'd screwed her over. Even before stealing the Star... From almost their first encounter, Finn had challenged her, made her question the existence her grandfather had built around her. He'd made her realize just how sheltered—and messed up—her family dynamic was. There was nothing quite like viewing your life through someone else's eyes, especially when they thought your life was shit.

At least that was one thing he'd given her. An understanding that she didn't have to accept the way her grandfather treated her. And the strength to demand more when the time had come...and walk away when her grandfather refused.

But that didn't negate the negative things Finn had also done. "I'm fully aware he has his own agenda and I have no intention of letting it affect my own choices or path."

Nick watched her for several seconds, the hard weight of his stare making her uncomfortable. She was afraid he could see right through her. She wanted the words to be true, but…she wasn't entirely certain they were. Yet.

She let out a silent sigh when he finally said, "Good."

Closing the gap between them, Nick wrapped his arms around her. There was something comforting about his hold. Supportive and protective, something she'd needed over the last few years. Nick had become the big brother she'd never had but always wanted.

"Go home. Get some sleep. I'll fix the window and we can tackle the rest tomorrow."

Nodding against his shoulder, Genevieve blurted out, "Noah and I are lucky to have you. Thank you for all you've done for us over the past few years."

His arms tightened for a second before he was pushing her away. "Go home."

Throwing him a grateful look, Genevieve didn't hesitate. She was exhausted and wanted nothing better than to crawl into bed and collapse.

Although sinking down into the warm leather seat of Finn's car didn't exactly make her feel comfortable. In fact, it made her jittery. Like what she was headed for was going to be just as difficult to deal with as what she'd left behind.

Finn stood in the middle of Genevieve's living room and stared. Her place was…*adequate* was probably the best word to describe it. Nothing special, other than the personal touches she'd used to make it her own, always with an artistic eye.

The artwork on her walls might not be the masters that had hung in the drawing room at her grandfather's estate, but they were beautiful. Abstract strokes of color that made him think of calm, quiet mountains and peace.

The sofa was overstuffed and appeared pretty comfortable. A far cry from the leather monstrosity her grandfather had insisted on. Functional, not there for the appearance of a welcome with the reality of being so uninviting that whoever sat down never stayed.

He'd taken the opportunity to wander through her home. Her kitchen was spotless and the pantry well stocked with what he assumed were baby essentials. Her clothes were neat and perfectly arranged, even if her wardrobe barely filled up a quarter of the walk-in closet.

And yes, it potentially made him a pervert, but he'd opened her drawers and run his fingertips over the soft silk of her panties. At least he hadn't stolen a pair.

Really, what he'd been looking for was something he could do for her. A chore he could take off her plate since she'd no doubt have plenty to worry about in the next couple days.

But there was nothing, not even a load of laundry waiting in a hamper.

He should have known, though; Genevieve was all about the details. He'd watched her work, not only the intricate designs she was creating now, but the body of pieces she'd created for Reilly over the years. She de-

signed with an intensity, focus and passion that was…
awe-inspiring. Not to mention tempting as hell.

Noah had barely stirred when Finn lifted his son
from his car seat, carried him inside and gently placed
him in his crib. He'd watched Noah's little body bur-
row deep into the mattress, his tiny butt wiggling for
several seconds until he'd found a comfortable position
and dropped back to sleep.

Now what? Without anything else to keep him oc-
cupied, Finn stood in the middle of Genevieve's living
room, a little at a loss.

Which wasn't comfortable at all.

He could imagine her here, curled up on her sofa, relaxed after a long day, with a glass of wine in her hand.
Or in the kitchen, barefoot, a huge smile stretching her
gorgeous lips as she stirred something delicious at the
stove. The subtle scent of her surrounded him, making
his blood whoosh faster in his veins.

This moment felt more intimate than he wanted it to
be. Like he was invading her space…and she was invading his mind.

Walking over to the sofa, Finn sank down, grabbed
the remote and turned the TV to some old Western
rerun, hoping it would offer a distraction.

And was asleep when Genevieve walked in a little
while later.

Genevieve had never felt so exhausted in her life.
Not even in those first few months after bringing Noah
home from the hospital, when she couldn't afford any
help and had been trying to do it all herself.

God, those first months had been rough.

But tonight…she was just bone weary. Mentally, emotionally and physically exhausted.

She wasn't prepared to walk through her back door only to be stopped dead in her tracks by the sight of Finn stretched out on her couch, the video screen from the baby monitor hugged against his chest like their son was there instead.

His face was turned away from her, but even in profile he appeared relaxed. Until that moment, she hadn't realized the complete change in him.

Before, Finn had always been relaxed. The man hadn't a care in the world. Only through hindsight had she realized nothing had been important enough to make him anxious or have him worry.

Now that the familiar expression had slackened his features, she realized Finn had been walking around carrying the serious weight of stress the handful of times she'd seen him since he'd returned.

Was it her? Noah? His time in prison? All of the above?

And did it really matter?

She didn't want it to, but maybe it did. *Crap.*

Kicking off her shoes and leaving them in a pile near the kitchen door, Genevieve padded across the room on quiet feet. Leaning over, she attempted to gently uncurl Finn's fingers from around the screen so she could take it to the bedroom with her.

Her plan was simply to leave him right where he was. It was damn late and only someone heartless would make him go home at this hour. Especially since he'd not only saved her studio, but taken care of her son so she could handle the fallout.

However, that plan didn't quite go as expected.

One second he was clearly asleep, the next his hand was wrapped around her wrist, and before she could blink, he'd pulled and had her tumbling across his hard body.

Genevieve let out a startled gasp. Her mouth landed against the warm curve of his throat, and before she could stop herself, her tongue darted out to steal a taste of his salty skin.

The soft angles of her body melted against his solid form. The hard band of his arm snaked around her waist, even as his fingers tightened their hold on her wrist.

His dark eyes glowed as he silently watched her, making heat spread through her entire body. Genevieve stared down at him, afraid to even breathe.

Slowly, he blinked. And just as quickly as she'd tumbled onto him, she found herself back on her feet. His fingers dragged against her skin, letting her go and taking several steps backward.

"I'm sorry, Genni. You startled me. Are you okay?"

Was she? Clearing her throat, she forced herself to say, "I'm fine. I didn't mean to startle *you*."

The warmth of his throaty chuckle washed across her senses. "I guess we both got a surprise."

That was one way to put it.

"Everything go okay with the police? They have any thoughts on who might have broken in?"

Genevieve's throat was bone-dry, but somehow she

was able to answer, "I don't really want to talk about it right now. What I need is to go to bed. No doubt Noah will be up bright and early like always. Toddlers wait for nothing and no one, not even late-night drama."

Instead of laughing at her lame attempt at humor as she'd expected, a frown pulled the space between Finn's gorgeous eyes. "I'll come over in the morning and handle Noah for you. You need some sleep."

God, yes, she did. But that probably wouldn't happen if Finn showed back up at her house tomorrow morning. Besides... "He's not something that needs to be handled."

His frown deepened. "I'm aware of that. You know what I meant."

"You've already helped enough."

"No, I haven't." Shaking his head, Finn started for her front door.

"Wait." *Goddammit.* What was she doing? "It's late. And something tells me whether I want you to or not, you'll be on my front porch right about sunrise."

He shrugged his shoulders.

"Stay. I'll make up the guest room. It's the least I can do after your help tonight."

Finn had been exhausted, but it was difficult to drop into sleep knowing Genevieve was down the hall. Especially after being woken up by the feel of her soft body falling against his.

It had taken everything inside him to set her back on her feet and not strip her naked so he could explore the luscious curves of her body.

So, he'd been restless and horny as hell. Which explained why he was groggy and bleary-eyed when he finally woke up the next morning. He didn't mind losing sleep…when it was necessary and worth it.

Rolling out of bed, he pulled on the pair of jeans he'd been wearing last night, not bothering with his Henley. If he'd been a gentleman, he would have. But that wasn't something he'd ever aspired to being.

And maybe there was a small part of him that wanted to know if Genevieve would still react to seeing him half-naked as she'd used to. He'd never been the kind of man to ignore an opportunity.

Padding out into the hallway, he listened for noise of some kind. Didn't babies like to cry and laugh and play?

But the place was eerily quiet.

Sticking his head inside Noah's room, Finn registered that the crib he'd laid his son in last night was empty. So was the office and the living room as he passed through.

The kitchen was empty, as well, although there was a coffee maker with an empty mug and an assortment of pods sitting on the counter just waiting.

His eyebrows beetled in confusion—had Genevieve left? He walked across to pop a pod in and start the drip of coffee into the waiting mug. Not that it would necessarily matter. She'd have to come home at some point. He could wait.

It wasn't until he crossed to the fridge for cream that he found her. Sitting outside on her back patio, legs curled up beneath her as she moved lazily on a swing. Her own mug was cradled between both palms and pressed against her chest, forgotten as she stared out across her open backyard.

God, he hated that expression on her face. Pensive and entirely too troubled. He recognized it from before. Usually only after she'd had a run-in with her grandfather. The man had the ability to take every spec of light that Genevieve harbored inside and snuff it out with a single well-directed, disparaging remark.

Her grandfather wasn't part of her life anymore, though, which made seeing it now almost worse. Now, just like back then, Finn had the undeniable urge to make the expression disappear at any cost.

Stepping through the back door, he joined her outside. The morning was crisp and cool. A slight salty tang hung in the air. Genevieve's backyard was nice, if on the small side. It was clearly set up for a child, with a swing set in the far corner and a sandbox up closer to the stone patio.

Genevieve didn't bother turning his direction when he walked up, although he knew she was aware that he'd come out. Her shoulders tensed, as if preparing for a fight.

Which was the last thing he wanted.

Sitting down next to her on the swing, he let his legs sprawl out, crowding into her personal space. "Where's Noah?"

"Where's your shirt?"

A quick shot of amusement tugged at the corners of his mouth. "You go first."

"My friend came and picked him up a little while ago."

Disappointment shot through him. He'd been looking forward to spending time with the both of them this morning. "Why?"

"It's our normal routine and I didn't see a reason to change it." For the first time since he'd walked out, she turned to him. Her gaze ripped down his body with the speed of a hummingbird's wings before jerking away again.

Interesting.

"Besides, I thought there were a few things we needed to discuss."

Without their son to distract either of them. Fine with him.

"I spoke with Nick this morning. He's preparing surveillance footage to give to the police."

"Excellent. I'll get my footage together, as well." Although he had every intention of keeping a couple of the cameras he'd installed to himself. The first rule of power was never reveal all your secrets.

This time when she looked at him her eyes were narrowed, but even as slits, Finn could see the shrewd calculation behind them. Genevieve might be naive, but she was far from stupid.

"And just why do you have footage to share? How did you know what was happening before Nick did?"

Finn took a quick sip of coffee and scalded his tongue. Stalling a little longer, he leaned forward and set the mug on the ground beneath them. "Do you really think I'd leave you and my son unprotected?"

She shook her head, her eyebrows crinkling with irritation and confusion. "What exactly do you think we need protection from? You're the most dangerous person in our lives."

That stung, although he really didn't think she'd meant it to.

"Obviously not, considering last night. You know better, Genevieve. You come from the world of privilege and money."

"None of that was ever mine."

"Maybe not, but not everyone understands. And plenty of people are aware who Noah's father is. If they weren't before, the public visitation proceedings fixed that. I might be a degenerate and an asshole, but I'm a filthy-rich one. And where there's money there are always people willing to take it."

"You'd certainly know," she mumbled under her breath.

If her words were intended to wound, they didn't. In fact, as far as he was concerned, she'd proved his point.

"Exactly. I take advantage of people's weaknesses. My philosophy has always been if you can't protect something, you don't deserve to own it."

"You don't own me or our son."

"No, I don't. But you and Noah are the most important parts of my life. And I won't let someone hurt you in order to get to me. I was never afraid of making enemies. I had plenty before I went to prison, and I made a few more while I was there."

Genevieve recoiled. "Are you saying Noah and I are in danger? Is there something I should be concerned about?"

"No, I'm just not willing to take any risks. I saw vulnerabilities in your security and I plugged the holes. And it turns out I was right, wasn't I?"

Finn watched Genevieve's jaw tighten and her eyes flash. "Instead of talking to me about it, you decided to take care of it yourself?"

He shrugged, unwilling to apologize for doing what he thought he needed to. "After the end run I had to do just to get a few thousand dollars into your hands... let's just say I didn't expect you to be receptive to either my observations or my footing the bill to correct the deficiencies. Like I said the other night, I have copies of your financials. You have no secrets from me, Genevieve."

Six

God, she hoped that wasn't true.

The last thing she needed was for Finn to know just how difficult it was to keep her hands to herself. Even pissed at him.

Damn him.

"Just because you might not like my answer doesn't give you the right to do whatever the hell you want, Finn. That's not how adult relationships work."

"Is that what this is, an adult relationship? Because if it is, I'd like to lodge a complaint. I'm not getting any of the adult perks."

How could the man make her body flush with heat at the same time she wanted to smack him across the face? "You know exactly what to say to get a rise out of me, don't you?"

"God, I hope so. Although I think you've gotten our anatomy confused again."

"You're incorrigible, and I'm still pissed at you."

Finn shrugged. "You can be pissed all you want. I won't apologize for protecting you and Noah."

Tipping her head back, Genevieve looked at the sky and prayed for patience. It didn't really help.

Pulling in a deep breath, she brought her focus back to Finn. "Were you going to tell me about the extra surveillance?"

"Eventually."

"Do I want to know when you thought that might be?"

"Probably not."

Well, she'd never said the man was stupid. In fact, he was too damn brilliant for his own good. Or hers, for that matter.

"But I need your permission to upgrade the system inside your studio, so sooner rather than later."

Letting out a frustrated sound, Genevieve gave up. Nothing she said would make a difference. Apparently, Finn could be stubborn as hell when he wanted to. Who knew?

"I think the words you're looking for are *thank you*."

"No, they really aren't." But weren't they? Even with his high-handed, sly tactics, Finn had saved her a lot of headache. Scrunching her nose up in distaste, Genevieve reluctantly said, "Fine. Thank you."

"Was that so difficult?"

Yes, it really was.

"You're welcome. While we're discussing security, I

should probably also let you know that I have a couple people analyzing the surveillance footage. While I'm certain they do the best they can, I don't necessarily trust our police force to put a ton of effort into finding a burglar who didn't actually steal anything."

Did she want to know who these people of his were? Apparently, she must have voiced the thought aloud because Finn actually answered.

"There are only a few people I'd trust with those most important to me. Stone and Gray are at the top of that list."

"Stone and Gray?"

"Anderson Stone and Gray Lockwood."

Of course she'd heard of both men. Anderson Stone had been in the media recently because of the controversy surrounding his own incarceration for manslaughter. And Gray Lockwood's embezzlement conviction had been watercooler fodder a few years ago.

"They're both better men than I could ever aspire to be."

Genevieve was surprised at Finn's confession, but found that hard to believe. It wasn't a point worth arguing over, though.

"They recently opened a security firm. They're both rich enough to be picky about the clients they take on and the cases they investigate. Right now, you're their only client."

"What do you mean I'm their only client?"

"Well, aside from working to prove Gray's innocence. I hired them to keep an eye on you and Noah."

Pushing up from the swing, Finn walked a few steps away. As Finn leaned his back against her porch railing, Genevieve couldn't stop herself from noticing the wide expanse of his hands, or the strength and dexterity of his fingers as he wrapped them around the long plank of wood behind him.

She remembered how he could make her feel with those fingers. The pleasure and excitement. With nothing more than a molten glance, Finn could make her feel desired, wanted. Sexy.

When she was with Finn, she saw herself differently. Because he'd seen her differently.

He'd convinced her that she deserved better than her grandfather's constant disapproval and criticism. She was smart and talented, but Finn was the first person in her life to convince her that was true.

To show her she was strong when she'd always thought herself weak.

"Why would you do that?" she finally asked, unsure she really wanted to know the answer.

"Because you and Noah matter to me. What will it take to make you believe me?"

Air backed up in her lungs. She wanted to tear her gaze from his, find her equilibrium so she could feel in control again. But he wouldn't let her go. His gaze was magnetic. Imploring. Tempting.

"I know I hurt you, Genni. And I know it can't take that pain away, but if it helps, I hurt myself, too."

"You're just saying that because I'm the first woman who's ever told you *no*. I'm the first one to resist."

Finn's head tipped sideways. A flash of something

crossed his face. It was so fast Genevieve didn't have time
to analyze or name it. But her belly certainly managed an
interpretation as it gave a slow roll. She was in trouble.

Before she could react, Finn was across the porch
and in her personal space. Reaching down, he grasped
her under the arms and lifted her up. His hard body
pressed into her from shoulder to hip.

Yep, big trouble.

Her body melted, traitor that it was, sinking into
his hold.

Leaning close, Finn brought his lips to her ear
and murmured, "Baby, don't lie. We both know you
wouldn't be able to resist if I put my mind to seduc-
ing you."

Her mouth opened to protest, but her brain shut down
the words before they could leave her lips. Because he
was right.

Even now, tiny tremors rolled through Genevieve's
body.

Tipping her head back, she stared up at him. Torn by
what she should do and what she wanted to do—which
was grab him and kiss the hell out of him.

She'd spent so much of her life afraid to do anything
but what she'd been told. She never broke the rules or
took any risk.

Until Finn.

He'd given her the confidence to be herself. And for
that she'd always be grateful, no matter what else happened between them.

But what good was that lesson if she chose to ignore
it when she was scared?

And everything about Finn DeLuca scared the hell out of her. Because nothing with him was simple or easy.

Her grandfather had ordered her to leave Finn alone. But for the first time in her life, she'd disobeyed. And look how that had turned out.

The weeks they'd shared had been a whirlwind of amazing. He'd made her feel special, powerful, beautiful. She'd taken a risk...and he'd betrayed her in the worst way.

After everything she'd been through, Genevieve had wanted to find a nice, quiet life with her son. No drama. No demanding men or complicated, forbidden love affairs.

She'd had that for the last couple years.

And she'd been bored out of her mind. She'd tried to convince herself that she hadn't needed or wanted the excitement Finn had shown her.

Such a lie.

Like a drug, she craved it. She craved him.

He'd awakened something inside her. And she was tired of denying what she wanted in order to do the right thing.

Who decided what was right, anyway?

Cupping her palms around Finn's jaw, she guided him down until their mouths touched.

And then she had no idea what to do next.

Finn's hands balled into fists at his hips. That was the only thing preventing him from snatching Genevieve up and hauling her hard against him.

But, God, he wanted to. He wanted *her*. And the fact that she'd been the one to initiate the kiss…amazing. And sexy as hell.

But a huge part of him wanted to see what she'd do next. How far would she take it?

Her hands landed lightly on his chest. She barely touched him, just skimming the surface as her fingers slid up his body. His dick shouldn't go half-hard from just that, but it did.

Rocking forward, Genevieve brought her body closer. Chest to belly, he could feel all of her soft curves and wanted them naked against his skin. Tilting her head, she changed the kiss, opened to him. Licked her tongue across his lips, asking for more.

He never wanted to deny her anything, least of all that.

Finn let himself sink into the kiss, although he was careful not to move. Because the minute he did…he didn't trust himself to keep control. He wanted her too much.

Instead, he watched her eyes drift shut. Her sigh brushed against his open mouth. Gorgeous. She was like the most precious work of art, vibrant and alive. He could stare at her for hours and never get bored. Not something he could say about much else in his life.

Most people bored the shit out of him. But never Genevieve, which didn't make any sense.

A tiny crease wrinkled the space right between her eyes. They fluttered open. She pulled back, breaking the physical connection between them. Her pale green eyes, huge and slightly unfocused, stared up at him as she asked, "What do you want from me?"

Everything. The word blasted through his brain. But

he was intelligent enough to prevent it from spilling from his lips.

"Right now? I want you to kiss me again. I want to pick you up, carry you inside and make love to you until we're both so exhausted we can't see straight."

Her sharp intake of breath dragged over him. Her pupils dilated and her body swayed closer. Triumph thrilled through him. She was teetering on the edge.

"But more than that, I want you to trust me."

And just as quickly as the dewy, distracted, sexy expression on her face had appeared, it vanished.

Well, shit.

Blowing out an annoyed breath, Genevieve swept a hand through her messy hair and took a step back. "Why couldn't you just stop at the sex?"

Her honest words surprised him, although they probably shouldn't. But he'd match her frankness just the same. "Because there's more between us. We have a son together and I want to be a part of his life."

"So you've said."

Finn chose to ignore the rueful tint to her words. "As much as I want you right now—and every time I'm within ten feet of you—I need more than amazing sex."

Palm against his chest, Genevieve put more space between them. She sank back into the waiting swing and pushed off with her feet. Every inch between them felt wrong, but the fact that she was still on the porch… For the first time since he'd watched the hurt and disappointment fill her face as the officer snapped handcuffs around his wrists, Finn wondered if there was a way back to what they'd had together.

Genevieve watched him, her eyes sharp as they searched his face in a way that made his skin feel too tight for his body. Slowly shaking her head, Genevieve finally said, "The problem is, I never know when you're giving me a line and when you're telling me the truth."

"I always tell you the truth, and I always will."

"Sure, just like you told me you were watching me."

Crossing his arms over his chest, Finn gave her a disappointed look. "Genni, you didn't ask me."

"Because it never occurred to me I needed to."

"Then you weren't paying attention and don't really know me."

Her lips twisting into a rueful grimace, she mumbled, "That's what I've been saying."

"Then let's fix that. Spend time with me and I'll tell you anything you want to know." Or, at least, the pieces he wanted her to know. His life contained plenty of shit he didn't want touching her. Things he'd never let taint her or his son.

He'd have to be careful, because he truly meant what he'd said. Finn never wanted to lie to Genevieve, but he understood the valuable use of creative omission. Ultimately, the more time they spent together, the more opportunities he had to win her trust. To prove she could let him into her and Noah's life without fearing he would betray her again.

"Have dinner with me tonight."

Her mouth opened and Finn could see the protest sitting there, right on her lips. But she didn't give it to him. Instead, she waited for several seconds before finally nodding her head. "Okay."

Moving fast, before she changed her mind, Finn pushed away from the railing and started back inside. "Perfect. I'll send a car for you at seven. In the meantime, Stone or Gray will probably be contacting you about upgrading the security system here at the house and at the studio."

Moving through the kitchen, Finn dropped his mug on the counter and scooped his keys off the hook where Genevieve had obviously left them last night.

Following quickly behind him, she grasped his arm and pulled him around to face her. "Wait. What?"

"Now that I have full access to your security system, I want to upgrade everything. Your equipment is seriously out of date. You're vulnerable."

Shaking her head, Genevieve said, "I didn't say you could have full access to anything."

Finn gave her a half grin. "Ah, but you didn't say I couldn't. Be smart, Genevieve. I'm the perfect person to spot the vulnerabilities and help correct them. Let me do this."

He could see the gears turning inside Genevieve's head as she considered. No doubt she was trying to figure out what he might have to gain. It sucked that he'd put doubt into her head. But it was impossible to change the past.

All he could do was work on what came next.

What is his angle?
Genevieve studied Finn, her brain whirling as she tried to come up with something…but there was nothing.

They both knew if he'd wanted to rob her blind he'd

had plenty of opportunity. So it wasn't money or the jewels in her safe. It definitely wasn't access to her grandfather's inventory since she no longer had that. He'd already won visitation with Noah and she'd been more than accommodating on that front.

She couldn't figure out how updating her surveillance system could benefit him.

Oh, she had no doubt Finn had a motive. He didn't do anything without a hidden agenda. She just hadn't figured it out yet.

Which scared her.

But she also couldn't argue with his logic. He was no doubt the best person to pinpoint her security weaknesses and suggest how to mitigate them. Hell, he'd probably logged at least a half dozen ways he could rob her blind after five seconds inside her studio.

She might not have known much about Finn DeLuca when he'd first come into her life. But afterward…she'd made it a point to learn as much as she could about her son's father. Her curiosity had nothing to do with the fact that she'd felt lost, vulnerable and idiotic after he'd used her. Nope, not at all.

But the information she'd uncovered—admittedly, with Nick's help—had been eye-opening. Stealing the Star of Reilly might have been the first time Finn had gotten caught, but he had quite the reputation within certain circles. Rumors and innuendo followed him right along with the trail of broken hearts he liked to leave behind.

He'd been on the radar of several law enforcement agencies, insurance companies and crime families.

However, the DeLuca name, seamlessly limitless purse strings, charm and devil-may-care attitude seemed to protect him from actual prosecution.

And the man didn't give a rip about rumor or innuendo. He didn't give a shit what anyone else thought of him.

Which was one of the qualities that had intrigued her about him in the first place.

And it still did.

He was so different from her in that respect. She envied him that quality, even as she realized he often took it too far to the other extreme.

However, watching him now, she had to wonder if going to prison had really and truly changed him.

The Finn she'd known before wouldn't have hesitated to take advantage of what she'd offered him. It hadn't escaped her notice that he'd obviously been interested. The hard length of his erection had been pressed tight against her belly.

Not to mention, he'd single-handedly saved her collection last night. She'd invested everything she had into these pieces and this show.

Crap. "Fine. Have your friends contact Nick."

Finn's jaw tightened. "No, I want them working with you directly. I don't trust Nick."

"Why? I've known him for years. Certainly longer than you. He worked with me at Reilly. He quit his job and followed me when I left. He's been a good friend. One of a handful of people I know I can count on."

"Are you really that blind?"

What the heck was he talking about? "What?"

"He's in love with you."

Genevieve scoffed. "No, he isn't. He's like my brother."

"You might see him that way, but trust me, that man wants in your pants."

Nope. "You're wrong. He's never made a single move."

"Which just means he's not certain of his reception." Closing the distance between them, Finn cupped her jaw, angling her face up to his. "Trust me, I know people. That man fancies himself in love with you. He relishes his role of protector and he isn't going to appreciate you getting advice or assistance from someone else. Especially if that someone is me. Nick will stonewall my people."

"No, he wouldn't. He'll recognize the value and appreciate the help. He's been a one-man show for a long time."

His fingers tightened on her jaw, gently urging her up onto her toes as he brought his own mouth down to connect with hers. The kiss was quick, but full of heat, stoking at the embers and making need flare through her hot and hard.

Murmuring against her lips, he said, "You really are naive. Luckily, it's one of the things I appreciate most about you," before stepping back and letting her go.

Genevieve's brain reeled, from both the kiss and Finn's words. How could the man take something that was clearly not a compliment and twist it until it became one?

God, he confused her.

"Stone and Gray deal directly with you," he reiterated in a tone that left no room for argument.

She really didn't have the time for that, but clearly Finn wasn't budging. "Whatever. But I've got a lot of work to do."

"Don't worry. The disruption will be minimal."

Yeah, right. Something told her Finn's definition of minimal and hers were probably two different things.

Seven

"I need your help." Finn didn't beat around the bush as he walked into Stone's office.

First, he knew his friend was going to agree. He, Stone and Gray had had each other's backs long enough that there was no doubt he could count on his friend for anything.

What was up in the air was whether Stone would provide the help for free, or if he was going to use this opportunity to extract a little payment.

He was a businessman, after all. And a damn good one.

Besides, that's how their world worked. A favor for a favor, even among friends.

Plopping into the chair across from the large mahogany desk his friend currently had his feet propped up on, Finn waited to find out.

Stone watched him for several seconds, his standard, blank expression on his face. That poker face had been one of Stone's biggest assets on the inside. No one knew what was going on inside that scarily brilliant mind of his. Not even his best friends.

Finn was no slouch when it came to intelligence. He'd received the best education money could buy. The rest of his knowledge he'd gained from hands-on experience. He was an excellent judge of character and understood how to intuit a person's desire to use it for his own advantage.

He'd never once been able to manipulate Stone. And it certainly wasn't for lack of trying. He did live for a challenge, after all.

After several seconds, a brilliant smile bloomed across Stone's face. "That's handy, because I need your help, as well."

So that was how he was going to play it.

"How did I know you were going to say that?"

"Because you're an intelligent man?"

"Uh-huh. Stop blowing smoke up my ass and tell me what this is going to cost me."

"Everything."

At least his friend was honest. That was one of the things he valued most about his friendship with Stone. He trusted the man implicitly, and that wasn't something he could say about many people.

Exactly three, in fact. Stone, Gray and Genevieve.

Finn let out a groan, already anticipating what Stone was going to say. "No."

"Yes."

"This is highway robbery."

"No, it's negotiation, and you're damn good at it. You walked in here fully aware of exactly what I was going to say."

That was true, but it didn't mean he couldn't protest. Loudly.

"You're being an idiot."

"No, I'm not."

"You know I want nothing to do with the business. You're going to extort—"

"Haggle."

Finn ignored Stone's interjection. "My participation. You realize that's a terrible way to gain cooperation. I have no incentive to care about the business. You're going to give me a chunk of your profits for nothing in return."

Stone laced his fingers behind his head and leaned farther back into his chair. A satisfied grin split his lips and Finn fought the very real urge to reach across the desk and deck him. The man could use a little crooked nose to make his pretty face less perfect.

"You forget, I know you better than just about anyone."

Oh, Finn wasn't forgetting anything.

"You like to pretend you're some debauched billionaire living the playboy lifestyle. However, we both know you work damn hard at something when you want to."

"Sure, but you fail to grasp that *I don't want to.*"

Stone shrugged. "Then it's my job to bring you something that piques your interest. Luckily, I have just the thing."

Of course he did. *Dammit.*

Shooting forward, Stone dropped his feet to the ground with a resounding thud. With quick, efficient movements, he snapped open a drawer, pulled out a folder and slid it across the desk toward Finn.

"The document is pretty straightforward, but feel free to have your lawyer take a look before you sign it."

Yeah, right. Finn wouldn't bother wasting the time. He had no doubt Stone had covered everything.

"You had this just ready and waiting?"

"Let's say I'm optimistically prepared."

"Asshole."

Flipping open the folder, Finn's gaze scanned the partnership agreement making him one-third owner in Stone Surveillance. No doubt the rest of it detailed the role each partner would play in the business, but it didn't really matter.

He'd do whatever his friends needed him to, which Stone had already been aware of. Finn didn't need to be a partner in order to help. But Stone had a need for the world to be fair, which was why he'd been hounding Finn for months to join the company.

It wasn't like Finn needed the money, although he had no doubt Stone Surveillance would become highly successful.

Without bothering to read the rest of it, Finn snatched up the heavy gold pen sitting on the desk and scrawled his name across the bottom of the last page. Flipping the folder closed, he shoved it back across to Stone.

"Happy?"

"Yep."

Well, that made one of them, but Finn wasn't going to argue with him anymore.

"I need you to get a team over to Genevieve's studio and home. The technology on her security system leaves a hell of a lot to be desired. I also need Gray to see if he can scrub the footage from last night to get more information. I want to know who the asshole is so I can beat him into the ground."

Stone pressed a button on the phone sitting on his desk, and Finn heard a beeping noise from the outer office. A few moments later a woman in her late thirties slipped into the room. She was pretty. Dressed conservatively and with a pleasant, accommodating smile on her face.

"Yes, Mr. Stone?"

Holding out the folder, Stone said, "Please make a copy of the document and bring it back for Mr. De-Luca."

Losing patience, Finn said, "I don't give a shit about the paperwork, Stone."

"I know, but I do."

The woman didn't even acknowledge the conversation. With a nod, she took the folder and disappeared back out the door.

Flipping his wrist over, Stone glanced at the heavy platinum watch. "A team's been at Genevieve's studio for about two hours now. They should have the equipment installed by late this afternoon. We'll move to her personal residence tomorrow. Gray should have a preliminary report by the morning, although he's already warned me there's not a lot to work with."

Finn frowned. "That doesn't sound like an amateur smash and grab."

"No, it doesn't," Stone agreed. But he didn't add anything else. And he wouldn't until he had definitive information to pass along.

In the meantime... "Thank you."

"You're welcome. I know she's important to you."

Finn's gaze narrowed. "My son is important to me, so yes, her safety and livelihood are important."

Stone didn't say anything, just raised a single eyebrow.

Finn wanted to argue, but he couldn't. For the first time since he'd watched a shadowy figure appear on the screen last night, he finally let his body relax.

"We've got you, Finn."

You'd think after several years he'd be used to that fact. But he wasn't. It had been a very long time since there'd been anyone in his life who unconditionally had his back. Not since Sawyer...

"Now, let me tell you how you can help us."

Genevieve tried to concentrate on the stones spread in front of her. Frowning, she moved them around. Again.

An itchy, restless sensation crawled beneath her skin. It was part frustration with the design she was supposed to be working on. Pushed up against a timeline that couldn't budge, she'd forced herself to start the setting for several of the smaller stones. But she wasn't happy. It just didn't feel right.

Unfortunately, she didn't have a better plan so she was moving forward, anyway. But the tedious work of preparing the settings, molding the platinum and gold, polishing them, measuring, marking and scoring for the gems…it was all time-consuming and she couldn't help but feel the time was wasted.

Adding to her level of frustration was the extra layer of edginess Finn's presence was causing her. If she'd known he would tag along with the team his friends had sent to upgrade her surveillance system, then she might have found a good reason to stay home.

Not that she could afford to lose a day of work.

Genevieve was at the microscope, using it to prepare a halo she was creating for one of the stones when a tremor bolted through her body. Her hands, usually rock steady when she was working, shook. The delicate instrument she was using jumped, scraping across the polished surface of platinum and leaving a mark.

"Dammit," she growled, pushing violently back from the expensive piece of equipment before she did something stupid and regretful. The casters on the bottom of her chair rattled as she rolled across the floor, but stopped suddenly when she crashed into something unexpected.

Or someone.

Finn's hands settled over her shoulders. "Easy there. What's wrong?"

What was wrong? Everything. Looking down at her hands in her lap, she realized they were trembling. And she still held the instrument she'd been using in a too-tight grip. Twisting to the side, she gently set the thing on the surface of a worktable and then shook out her hand.

Pushing up from the chair, she pivoted and moved

out from beneath Finn's grip. Right now, she didn't want him to touch her.

Or she wanted him to touch her too much. She was no longer certain which one.

"What's wrong?" she repeated his question, still uncertain exactly what to say.

She wanted to yell at him. To tell him he was the problem. He and his friends who'd been in her space for the last couple days. Disrupting her work, sending Nick into a tizzy and making her life generally more complicated.

But that wasn't exactly fair. Sure, the mistake she'd just made—one that would set her back several hours of work—wasn't his fault. Even if his presence had been the reason for the jolt through her body.

Genevieve had known the moment he walked into the studio. Her body responded. Wanted.

Damn him.

Licking a tongue across suddenly dry lips, she answered in the only way that wouldn't reveal too much. "Just a problem with the design."

Holding out a hand, he said, "Let me see."

"No."

A single dark eyebrow winged up and he waited, hand outstretched. Several tense seconds pulled between them. Finally, with a frustrated sigh, she reached behind her, snatched the piece up and slapped it against his palm.

Squinting, he brought it close so he could inspect the setting. His lips pursed as he turned it. Finally, he closed a fist around it and dropped it to his side.

"Aside from the scratch, it's good work."

Genevieve nodded, expecting nothing less. But he didn't stop there.

"Your heart isn't in this."

No, it wasn't. "I know."

"Then why are you working on it?"

"Because I don't have a choice. I need to finish the piece and there isn't enough time if I don't get to work on it now."

Reaching for her, Finn wrapped his hands around her arms and gently pulled her close. The warmth of his body was so tempting, especially when he just held her for several seconds. Tucking her head against his chest, he rested his chin on the crown of her head. Together, they stood there and breathed.

And for the first time in weeks a sense of calm washed over her.

Pulling in a deep breath, Genevieve held it for several seconds before blowing it out on a long streaming sigh.

Shifting, Finn pushed her out to arm's length and guided her over to one of the high stools she kept in the studio. Edging her down onto it, he said, "Show me the design."

Genevieve shook her head. "I don't have one."

"Why not?"

It was a valid question. Normally, she started with a sketch, transferred the idea into a program on her computer that set the dimensions of the entire piece and allowed her to make adjustments down to millimeters.

The problem was, none of the sketches she'd done had felt good enough to move to the program. But she'd been out of time so decided to use the old-school method and just wing it. Part of her had hoped inspiration would strike while she was working with the stones.

Clearly, that wasn't happening.

Finn watched Genevieve's internal struggle. Disappointment, desperation and anxiety crossed her beautiful face. His first thought was how he could fix the problem for her.

Finally, she shrugged her shoulders. "None of the designs felt right. But I don't have time to wait for inspiration. I need to get started on the piece or it'll never be ready in time."

"Show me."

Shaking her head, Genevieve said, "This isn't your problem."

Maybe not, but he wasn't about to leave her frustrated and unhappy when there was potentially something he could do about it. "Show me."

Wrinkling her nose, she finally turned to the large safe mounted on the far wall of her workroom. Finn didn't bother to look away as she entered the combination on the keypad. Mostly because knowing the code wouldn't make a damn bit of difference. If he'd wanted inside it would have taken him less than ninety seconds. Upgrading the thing was next on his list.

The heavy door creaked, metal scraping against metal, as Genevieve swung it wide. Inside, there were several shelves and drawers. Reaching for one in the middle, she pulled it fully out of the safe. Cradling it in her arms, she turned to the worktable and set it down.

Stepping closer, Finn peered down at the seven stones spread across the black velvet.

He wasn't sure what he'd expected, but the deep purplish-red of the alexandrite wasn't it. In artificial light some people mistook the gems for rubies, but Finn knew immediately what Genevieve had.

Grabbing the biggest stone—at least three carats and worth probably around thirty thousand depending on the gem's ability to shift color—he walked across the room. The stone was cool in his palm. He couldn't help but move his hand up and down in an unconscious attempt to pinpoint the weight.

Thrusting it into the natural light streaming in from the floor-to-ceiling window, the gem shifted to a deep turquoise color that had breath backing into his lungs. "Gorgeous," he breathed.

Alexandrite might not be as expensive as diamonds, but it was rarer. Especially at this quality.

Even engrossed in the stone, he knew Genevieve was standing right beside him. Her soft, floral scent washed over him, filling his head and making his blood whoosh. The need for her was always right there, churning beneath the surface.

"Do all the other stones have this depth of color?"

Reaching out, Genevieve ran a soft fingertip over the beveled surface. "Yes."

And he was immediately half-hard, needing her to touch him in the same reverent way.

Nope, now was not the time.

"The stones are gorgeous. Seductive. Why is it so hard to find the right design?"

Finn didn't think her distracted question was actually directed at him. It was clearly an internal one, and one she'd asked herself before with no real answer.

Closing his fist around the stone, Finn registered the way it absorbed his body heat, soaking in warmth just as it did the light.

Genevieve's gaze skipped up to his. The way she looked at him... Finn's chest tightened, trepidation and need twisting into a painful band.

"We'll figure this out," he promised, reaching up and running a finger down the soft slope of her jaw.

She blinked, unconsciously leaning into his touch. "I've had the stones for two months. I haven't figured it out yet."

"I wasn't here." Finn flashed her a self-deprecating smile and started walking backward.

Genevieve let out a groan and rolled her eyes. "Your ego is enormous."

Finn's grin grew. He kept backing toward the work-table and after several seconds she followed. When his back bumped against the edge, he turned to set the gem onto the black velvet.

Picking up each of the other stones, he studied them for several seconds before placing them next to the largest. Genevieve slid up beside him, her tiny, talented hands gripping tightly to the edge of the table.

Once the gems were displayed, Finn tilted his head and looked at them as a whole.

"One piece or several?"

"The smart move is a necklace, earrings and bracelet."

"Sure." That made sense. She had enough stones of

varying sizes to make a set. But it was expected and safe. Two words the world might use to describe Genevieve… but that was only because they didn't really know her.

Not like he did.

In many ways, Genevieve was just like the gems she worked with. Polished and perfect on the outside. But on the inside…only the best gemstones held fire.

"Why do you need to make the safe choice?"

"Because I have a business and brand to build. I have a son to support. I need to make smart choices."

Hearing her say those words made him cringe. Genevieve had spent a lifetime making smart choices. But that was such a bland existence. He better than anyone understood that living a perfect life didn't necessarily mean safety, happiness and longevity.

Sawyer had been the angel to Finn's devil. And look at what had happened to him…

"In this case, I think playing it safe is working against you. These stones scream for something outrageous and amazing. They need to be the jewels in someone's crown."

"I'm designing for the commercial market. Yes, these pieces are custom, but each piece will inspire pieces that can be sold and marketed in each of the Mitchell Brothers' stores. Not many women need a crown."

"I'm perfectly aware of how your arrangement is supposed to work." And not just simply because he'd gotten his hands on a copy of her contract with the brothers and had his own legal team review it. "But you already have several pieces that accomplish that goal. What you don't have is a centerpiece you can use to make a media splash at the premiere."

In the right design, Finn had no doubt these stones would make everyone salivate. They were unexpected, but so gorgeously seductive.

"I have so much money tied up in the stones. I need the piece to sell, not just cause a scene."

"How about this, I promise if no one else shows interest, then I'll buy it."

This time when Genevieve frowned, it was directed straight at him. He felt the impact of her irritation, but let it roll right off him.

"You promised you wouldn't buy any more of my pieces just for the sake of getting me money."

Shifting closer, Finn let his fingertips slip down the line of her jaw. Her skin was so soft and smooth. A warm contrast to the cool gem he'd held just moments ago. Using the pressure of his finger, he tipped her chin up.

Her eyes dilated and her pink lips parted. She unconsciously leaned closer, begging him to kiss her.

Instead, he maneuvered so he could stare straight into her pale green eyes. "When will you understand I don't do anything I don't want to? I want to take care of you and Noah."

"We don't need to be taken care of."

"I'm aware. Doesn't prevent me from wanting to do it. I also want these stones. They're gorgeous. I happen to have faith that the design you come up with will be amazing. If nothing else, purchasing them will be a wonderful investment."

"You have more faith in me than I do right now."

Eight

What was it about the man that cut straight through all of her defenses?

His fingers slipped across her skin, sending a wave of goose bumps down her arms. Genevieve stared up at him, utterly drowning in his deep brown eyes.

"Genevieve, I have no doubt you can accomplish anything you set your mind to. But if you need my faith in you right now until you can find your own…you're welcome to it."

Hell. The words coming out of his mouth were a line. But the expression in his eyes was pure sincerity. Her brain told her not to fall for it. The rest of her wanted to dive headfirst into him.

"If you weren't thinking about commerciality, what would you do?"

Genevieve stared at the stones, thoughts and ideas flying through her brain. As soon as one popped up, though, she automatically dismissed it without giving it voice.

"No, don't censor. Tell me."

"I could do a larger necklace with intricate filigree. Use smaller diamonds to accent. Platinum and white gold for the settings. The metals would contrast the deep, rich colors in the stones."

"Yes, they would. Draw it up."

Genevieve shook her head. "No one needs a necklace like that. When I designed those kind of statement pieces at Reilly they were always commissioned. The cost of the materials is just too much without a buyer. Especially right now."

"You have a buyer. Draw it up."

What was she going to do with him? He was offering her the opportunity to do exactly what she wanted. If she was honest, the design had been in the back of her mind from the moment she first saw the stones. The reason no other design had worked was because they weren't *that* one.

She shouldn't want anything from Finn DeLuca. So why did she want to let him give her everything?

Making up her mind, Genevieve turned to him. "Fine. I'll draw it up tonight, show you tomorrow for approval."

"You don't need my approval for anything, Genni."

Yes, she did. She was going to treat this like any other commissioned piece. Because if she didn't, what she was about to do would make her feel...edgy and restless. "Maybe not, but since you're the buyer, you get approval."

"Fine."

That settled, she shifted closer. Going up on her tiptoes, Genevieve wrapped her hands around his face and tugged. His body bent as hers lifted, coming together with a whoosh of breath and an overwhelming feeling of right.

Her mouth found his, angling to give them both access. The kiss started out soft and hesitant. Because Genevieve was in charge and she wasn't entirely certain of her reception.

Sure, Finn had kissed her the other day, but since then…he'd made no move to touch her again. His lack of interest had been frustrating, not to mention a little soul crushing. Part of her was waiting for him to pull back, set her away from him and gently tell her he wasn't interested in blurring the lines.

But she shouldn't have worried.

Sliding her hands down his body, over the tight expanse of chest, to rest on his hips, Genevieve relished the feel of him. She wanted more. Memories of their time together flashed across her mind. Hot, sweaty nights. The way he'd made her feel powerful, beautiful, alive. The expression on his face as his gaze raked across her naked body…like he couldn't breathe without her.

She wanted that again. Was greedy for it.

No one in her life had ever made her feel the way Finn DeLuca could. Maybe it was stupid, but she was going to grab that while she had the opportunity. For however long it lasted.

There'd be time enough to deal with the complications that came with her decision later. Right now, she just wanted him. Wanted them.

Gripping the hem of his shirt, Genevieve tugged it out of the waistband of his slacks so she could find his naked skin. A tortured hiss slipped from his parted lips when her hands found their target.

She relished the way his fingers flexed where they gripped her own hips. Involuntary reaction. Genevieve liked knowing she wasn't the only one a little out of control.

What she wasn't prepared for was for Finn to use the hold to lift her up into the air. She let out a yelp of surprise, scrambling for something to hold on to. Her hands landed on his shoulders, gripping tight. After a few seconds of air time Finn settled her onto the worktable.

Nudging her thighs wide with a knee, he stepped up against the table and settled into the open V. His hands tangled into the hair at her nape, using his hold to tilt her head for another kiss.

She didn't have a chance to take a breath before he was devouring her. Silently demanding she open to him and give him whatever he wanted. A thrill raced along Genevieve's skin.

God, he made her feel alive.

Reaching behind him, Finn gathered a handful of shirt into his fist and pulled it up over his head. Standing half-naked before her, she couldn't resist laying her hands on him.

The wide expanse of his chest and shoulders tapered down at his hips. The man had always been built, but clearly he'd put his time in prison to good use. He now sported layers of muscle that definitely hadn't been there before.

Running her hands over him, Genevieve let her fingertips explore the dips and valleys. Flicking a fingernail over the tight peak of his nipple, she relished the hiss he let out. Her gaze followed the trail of her fingers, studying, cataloging, exploring.

Leaning forward, she placed her mouth on his skin and let her lips join the fun. His skin was warm, the taste of him a combination of salt and spice that made her tongue tingle.

"God, you taste good," she murmured.

His grip on her tightened. Thumbs beneath her chin, he tipped her gaze up to meet his again. His body was still, but with her hands on him, she could feel the tension snapping through him.

Calculated exactly how much he was holding back.

"Now's the time to say stop."

No. The single word screamed through her brain. "Don't stop."

"No regrets."

It wasn't a question. He was telling her that whatever happened from here was her choice. At this moment the power was all hers.

Genevieve shook her head. "No."

Apparently, that was all the answer he needed. Reaching into the collar of her blouse, Finn pulled it in two. Buttons popped, pinging against the wall, table and floor. He didn't even bother to apologize for ruining it before he was pushing it over her shoulders and away. The soft fabric fluttered into a puddle on the table.

But Genevieve didn't have time to care. Reaching behind her, Finn popped the clasp of her bra, sliding it down her arms and tossing it behind them.

Cool air ghosted across her naked skin. Her nipples tingled and tightened, and not just from the change in temperature. The heat in Finn's gaze scraped across her exposed body, sending a rush of awareness down her spine.

His features sharpened with need. A need that reverberated through her own body.

Her fingers shook as she scrambled to find the opening to the fly of his slacks. With impatient fingers, Finn brushed her away and finished the job himself. The buckle of his belt clanged as it hit the floor. Genevieve watched him toe off his shoes and kick everything out of the way.

The hard length of his desire jutted out from his hips. Long, swollen and a dark, tempting red at the tip. Genevieve wanted to lean forward and suck him deep, but when she shifted to do just that, he stopped her.

Instead, he found the zipper to her own jeans. Leaning her back and supporting her with an arm at her back, Finn pulled her pants down and off, leaving her naked. Exposed.

Aching.

Using her prone position to his advantage, Finn used a palm to the middle of her back to hold her in place. His mouth found her, starting at the curve where her neck met her shoulder. Following the line of tendon, he nipped and sucked.

Genevieve's eyes closed at the pleasure.

But he didn't stop there. His lips trailed fire over her shoulder and collarbone. Circling and teasing down in a pattern that came close, but didn't quite touch where she wanted him most.

She fought the urge to squirm, but ultimately lost the battle. Panting and shifting, trying to move her body so he couldn't avoid her tight, achy nipples anymore.

An involuntary cry shot out when he finally gave her what she wanted. His lips closed around a tight bud, drawing it deep. His cheeks hollowed out as he sucked, using the edge of his teeth to scrape the sensitive flesh.

Transferring his attention to the other, he let his teeth close around the pouting pink nub. Gently, he tugged, applying the perfect pressure to have her head dropping back, enjoying the amazing sensations he stirred inside her.

But he didn't stop there. His mouth continued the trail down her body. A palm to the center of her chest, Finn urged her down. The black velvet felt soft, rich, decadent against her overly sensitized skin.

Using the flat of his tongue, he licked up the crease where her hip and thigh met. The unexpected sensation had her hips bucking off the table.

Dropping to his knees, Finn placed a hand on either knee and pushed gently until she opened wider. It wasn't the first time he'd had a front-row view to her sex. But it had been long enough that a moment of unease shot through her.

She'd given birth since the last time they'd had sex. Her body had changed in ways she hadn't even thought about until right now.

"Relax," Finn murmured, the single word brushing against her heated skin.

Easy for him to say.

But two breaths later her own self-consciousness melted away. Because his mouth found her.

The sharp tip of his tongue swiped across her sex. He found her clit and, using the flat of his tongue, laved it over and over again.

Sparks shot through her body, repeatedly popping. Every muscle drew tight, straining closer and closer to the relief only he could give her.

Using his thumbs, Finn spread the lips of her sex wide, giving him better access to torture her. Genevieve bucked and whimpered. Finn growled, the rumble of sound vibrating through her in a way that left her gasping.

"Give it to me, Genni. Let me watch you come."

Her body had always been eager to do anything he asked.

The tight rope of tension snapped. Her body spasmed. Pleasure washed over her, a wave that quickly pulled her under. Genevieve knew nothing except the feel of Finn's hands and mouth as he pushed her to ride out the orgasm, followed her down, chasing for more.

Reality returned slowly, in bits and pieces. Except that the world was still dark. It took her several seconds to realize her eyes were closed.

When they popped open it was to find Finn looming over her. Watching her. A satisfied grin curled the corners of his lips.

But his dark eyes… God, they made her sex clench again, another tremor rocking through her.

"Why do you look like the cat that ate the canary when I'm the one who just had a mind-blowing orgasm?"

"Mind-blowing, huh?"

Genevieve smacked his shoulder. "Don't be an ass. You know damn well you just rocked my world."

"Yeah, but a guy likes to hear the words, anyway. And just so we're clear, I'm not done with you yet."

Heat and need swirled through his expression, sending a thrill down her spine.

She wanted that. All of it. How could she crave more with the power of what he'd just given her?

Finn couldn't take his eyes off her. Genevieve was gorgeous. Flushed. Disheveled, and he liked knowing he was the reason she looked that way.

He couldn't help but compare the girl she'd been to the woman she was now. Three years could make such a difference. The first time he'd made love to her, she'd been shy and uncertain. Now, she was confident and unapologetic. Spread before him across her worktable, she didn't even attempt to cover her nakedness.

In fact, he watched her stretch, her back arching up and her breasts thrusting closer to his face. "You're not done with me yet, hmm?"

"Tease," he growled.

"I'm pretty sure you can only use that word if there's no follow-through."

She wanted to play games, did she? Games he enjoyed.

Backing up, he decided to see just where she planned on going with this. His little temptress.

"Feel free to show me your follow-through, sweetheart."

The view didn't suck, either, as he took several steps away. The black velvet beneath Genevieve's body made the alabaster of her skin glow. Yellow-gold light streamed down from above, highlighting the luscious curves of her body. Her red-gold hair shone like fire.

A knowing smile pulled at the corners of her mouth as she watched him back away. Her eyelids lowered, giving him a sleepy, sexy expression that immediately went to his dick.

The tempting pink tip of Genevieve's tongue slowly licked across her bottom lip. Excruciatingly slowly, she spread her thighs wide, inch by inch, revealing what he'd been dreaming about for the last three years.

His memories didn't do her justice.

Genevieve's sex glistened with the evidence of her orgasm. She was slick and swollen. And he wanted to sink into her. To feel the tight walls of her grasping at him, pulling him deeper.

Bracing on one arm, she let her hand drift across her body. Her teasing fingers plucked at the tight pink bud of her nipple before trailing down her belly, over her hips and back up the inside of her thighs.

She was teasing them both.

Her head dropped back, but she didn't break eye contact with him. She wanted him to watch.

Stroking the lips of her sex, she let out a tiny gasp when she found the sensitive nub of nerves. Her hips jerked as she rolled her thumb over and over that perfect spot.

Finn wasn't certain at what point he'd gripped his aching cock, but the sensation of his own palm rubbing up and down the hard length was both excruciating and heaven.

Because it wasn't enough.

And he wasn't about to go off in his own hand when he had Genevieve spread like a gift in front of him.

A strangled sob caught in her throat as she plunged two fingers deep inside her own sex. Her eyes slid shut. That broken connection was enough to have him moving.

In two strides, he was back between her spread thighs. His hands were probably rough as he grasped her hand, flinging it away from her body. She didn't seem to care. And he was fresh out of finesse.

Genevieve reached for him, her fingers digging into his hips as she urged him closer.

"Please, Finn," she whimpered.

The sound of his name on her lips in that begging tone did wicked and weird things inside him. He'd do anything she wanted. She made him want to be a better man. The kind she deserved.

But she also made him want to growl and shout from the highest rooftop that she was his. She made him sloppy. She made him give a damn, which was dangerous.

How could she make him want to be both the best and the worst versions of himself at the same time?

Not that it really mattered. It simply was. Genevieve was complicated, and his reaction to her was even more so.

Caught up in her own cloud of need, she reached for him. Her fingernails dug into his skin. The pinch helped to center him, bring him back to the here and now.

Curling his body over hers, Finn placed his palms on either side of her. Finding her mouth, he pulled the taste of her deep inside.

His dick throbbed with need, but he had to ask a couple questions first.

Staring into her glassy eyes, he asked, "Are you on something?"

"Huh?"

"Birth control. As much as I want you pregnant again so I can experience everything with you this time, I think probably not a smart move."

"Oh." She blinked, the haze clearing a little. "Yeah, I'm on the Pill."

Thank God. "Obviously, I'm clean."

She blinked again. "Oookay."

Perfect. Bending his head, Finn tugged the bud of her nipple into his mouth. Grasping her hips, he pulled her to the edge of the table so that he could align his cock with the tight, wet entrance to her body.

Genevieve's hands curled over his shoulders. "Wait. Wait."

Finn stilled, the head of his dick kissing the moist heat of her pussy. It was torture to stand there, so close to heaven, but he did.

Closing his eyes, Finn started to back away, but Genevieve's legs wrapped around his hips tightened, keeping him in place.

"You aren't going to ask me if I'm clean?"

That's what she was worried about?

Finn could count his own heartbeat as it pulsed through his cock. The opening to Genevieve's sex fluttered around the tip. She pulled his hips closer, and it was just too much.

Using his grip on her, Finn pulled her forward at the same time he thrust deep. He slipped inside her body like he was born to be there. A groan of relief rumbled up through his chest. Genevieve let out a matching sigh.

The walls of her sex clamped down around him, squeezing tight and stealing his breath.

"Holy shit." The words just popped out.

Wrapping his hands around her face, Finn said, "Look at me."

Genevieve's heavy-lidded gaze snapped to his.

"I didn't ask because I already knew the answer. How many times do I have to tell you that I know exactly what you've been doing for the last three years? Genevieve, you and Noah matter. You have from the moment I laid eyes on you."

She shook her head. "Too much."

She was wrong. "Not enough," he countered.

This was a discussion they could have later. Right now, he needed to feel her fall apart in his arms.

Using his leverage, Finn began to thrust in and out of her body. Slowly at first, relishing the pleasure he found from her. The excruciatingly satisfying scrape and pull of friction.

Genevieve whimpered. She spread her thighs wide, rocking her hips in time with his movements. Gripping his shoulders, she held on.

It had been a damn long time since he'd had sex. Since the last time he'd touched her. Before, a dry spell for him had been going three days without a woman in his bed, let alone over three years.

"This isn't going to last long," he warned.

Her response was to lean forward, sink her teeth into his shoulder and shatter around him. The wave of her orgasm broke over him, sucking him under.

The world spiraled down into a darkness that left only Genevieve at the center. His own release started at the base of his spine and shot straight out in hot spurts that left him gasping and weak.

His knees sagged against the table and his arms collapsed out from under him. If it wasn't for Genevieve's thighs wrapped tight around his body he might have hit the floor. Instead, he ended up draped half across her body and half across the table.

His harsh breathing mixed with hers. Her head was buried against the column of his throat.

He was aware enough to register the flutter of her mouth as she placed a kiss against his skin.

Yes. This was right.

Finding strength from somewhere, Finn rolled back up onto his feet. He scooped her into his arms, spun to find the office chair on the far side of the room and collapsed down, cradling her naked body against his.

After a few seconds, Genevieve stirred. Shifting, she looked up at him, an impish grin tugging at her lips.

"You finished with me now?"

"Not even close."

Nine

Genevieve woke up alone. She knew Finn was gone before she'd even opened her eyes. Dread curled through her belly, but she forced it down. Nope, she wasn't going to let herself think the worst.

But instinct had her hand moving over to where he'd been sleeping to test if the sheets held any residual warmth. They did, although what did that prove?

Nothing really, except that she needed to get a grip on herself. She was either doing this or she wasn't, and if she was she couldn't live every day waiting for the other shoe to drop.

That wasn't fair to Finn, but it also wasn't fair to Noah. Or herself.

Rolling onto her back, Genevieve pressed the heels of her palms into her eyes and rubbed. It had been two days since the studio. And since then, Finn had been at her side. Which was amazing, but it was also overwhelming.

She hadn't had a chance to catch her breath. To reason her way through what was happening and just how she needed to handle it all.

Maybe she needed to send Finn home for a while.

Grabbing her phone from the nightstand, Genevieve looked at the screen through bleary eyes, but that all changed when she registered the big numbers glaring at her.

9:18.

Bolting out of bed, she was halfway down the hall, her heart thudding for a completely different reason. No toddler slept until 9:18. Something was wrong.

It didn't help to find her son's room empty. Or for the rest of the house to feel eerily quiet. Darting through the house, she skidded to a halt at the kitchen. The empty kitchen.

Spinning in a circle, the dread that had churned her belly minutes before was now making it a whirlpool. Until something out of place caught her eye. A white piece of paper in the middle of the counter.

Snatching it up, her eyes raced over the words, just starting to digest them as the garage door began to rumble.

Yanking open the door, she raced into the garage. Even though, thanks to Finn's note, her brain knew what was going on, the rest of her needed to feel Noah's little body cradled in her arms.

Finn had barely stopped the car before Genevieve

popped open the back door. Noah grinned up at her, chocolate smeared across his angelic face.

"Doughnuts, Mama."

Her precious son took the smashed-up treat gripped in his tight fist and shoved it against her lips.

Her hands shook as she unbuckled him from his seat. Her arms felt weak, but she wasn't about to let him go once she'd scooped him up. Hugging him close, Genevieve pressed a kiss to his head and breathed in his toddler scent.

Rounding the car, Finn gave her a huge grin and leaned in for a kiss. But after touching his lips to hers he suddenly pulled back. His eyebrows beetled with confusion.

"Hey, what's wrong?"

With his arm wrapped around her body, there was no way she could hide the tremors still working through her.

"I woke up and you were both gone." She should have stopped there, but words tumbled out. "He's my whole world and I don't know what I'd do if you took him away from me."

Finn jerked backward as if she'd hit him. Which only made the sludge of nasty emotions in her belly worse.

Shaking his head slowly, he said, "I would never take him away from you. Not ever, but definitely not like that."

"I know." The minute the words were out of her mouth, she realized they were the truth. Finn was a con artist and a thief. But he had his own twisted sense of honor. He'd done nothing but help her since he'd forced his way back into her life. And while she might not trust him implicitly, she did trust him to protect their son.

Closing her eyes, Genevieve realized how terribly she'd just screwed up. Reaching for him, she placed her hand along the hard ridge of his jaw. "I'm sorry. You didn't deserve that reaction."

"No, I didn't." His words were harsh, but the hand he pressed into the small of her back was gentle. "But I understand."

She seriously doubted that he did. But even if so, that didn't make what she'd just done any less regrettable.

It was clear, by the expression in his eyes, that she'd hurt him. Something she wouldn't have thought possible.

Finn DeLuca didn't let anyone matter enough to inflict pain. Or he hadn't before. Even when she'd thought he was letting her in, it became obvious to her in hindsight that while she'd opened up to him about her worst fears, deepest secrets and most private desires…he'd given her absolutely nothing. In fact, he'd used what she had shared with him in order to get exactly what he wanted.

For the first time, Genevieve stopped being pissed because that reality had left her vulnerable, devastated and feeling like a stupid idiot. Instead, she started to wonder *why*.

What had happened to make Finn DeLuca the man he was? A charming, egotistical, devilish loner?

She had no idea what this was between them, and wasn't willing to even ask the question at this point. But what she did know was that this time she wasn't going to let him get away with keeping himself separate and walled away.

Genevieve had every intention of demanding more.

It was the middle of the night. Finn, Genevieve and Noah had spent all day together. After the rocky start in the morning, it had turned into an amazing day.

Made even better by the fact that Genevieve was naked, spread out diagonally across the bed, her hair a mess, her skin flushed from pleasure and a relaxed smile on her face. The orgasms he'd had didn't suck, either.

Propped up on an elbow, she watched him. "Tell me something I don't know."

Such a typical Genevieve demand. "That's a pretty wide area to cover. And a difficult order to comply with. I don't know everything you know so I can't fill in the gaps."

She kicked out, her foot connecting lightly with his shoulder. "You know what I mean."

"No, I really don't."

"Tell me something about you I don't know. Before, you didn't share anything. You've said several times that I have no secrets—which is creepy, by the way. You have nothing but secrets. I know you're wealthy, but I don't know how or why. I know you like jewels and art, but I don't know where that desire started from. I don't know if you have any family. Brothers, sisters, parents?"

A frown tugged at the corners of her mouth. She rolled, grabbing the sheets and tucking them around her body. As if cataloging all the things she didn't know about him made her feel exposed.

Nope, he wasn't going to let her start hiding from him now.

Reaching out, Finn grasped the edge of the covers and yanked. They dragged against her skin, slithering against her body as he tossed them onto the floor beside them.

"Hey," she exclaimed, leaning up and chasing after them.

Finn snaked an arm around her waist, tugging as he tumbled them both back to the bed.

She struggled for a few seconds and he let her, waiting until she'd calmed again before rolling them so she was tucked into the curve of his body.

"I have family money. My great-great-grandfather owned a plantation. He grew cotton and tobacco. But my great-grandfather wanted to move away from agriculture and slavery, and he wanted to be more powerful and influential. He used the family connections to build an import/export business, eventually building a transportation conglomerate. Shipping, rail, trucking, each generation managed to grow the business...until it became a multibillion-dollar corporation."

Genevieve's fingers began to play against his chest, lightly stroking his skin in a way that was soothing and arousing at the same time.

"My father was no exception. He spent his entire life devoted to growing the company. However, his focus was on expansion, which meant he was always traveling. Gone for months at a time as he opened a new hub in Europe or Asia. Or acquired some tiny warehouse in Africa. My mom went with him."

Finn heard the bitterness in his own voice and hated himself a little for it. You'd think after so many years he would have gotten past the anger. Apparently, not so much. "They were rarely home, and when they were they spent most of their time at the office. The business was their life."

"Is that why it's not yours?"

"Partly." No, that wasn't true. "Absolutely. I didn't learn much from my parents, but I did learn that life requires balance. Sawyer and I decided early on we weren't going to let the company—or any job—consume us the way it did my parents."

"Sawyer?"

Tension tightened his shoulders. Finn consciously tried to relax it away, but it didn't help. "My little brother."

"Where is he? When do I get to meet him?"

"He's dead."

Genevieve shifted, trying to move so she could look up at him. Tightening his arms around her, Finn kept her right where she was.

"How?"

Of course she'd ask. Finn fought against the rage that always tried to swallow him whole whenever he thought about Sawyer. The problem was that whenever he won the battle, that just left the guilt. The guilt he'd never be able to get rid of.

"I was an adrenaline junkie when I was younger."

Genevieve tipped her head sideways. The fingers that had been playing across his skin stalled for several seconds. No doubt she was confused how his statement answered her question.

"The problem with having no goal in life, but enough money at your disposal to buy whole islands, is that you get bored."

"Not necessarily. *You* got bored."

"Fair enough. I got bored. It didn't take me long to figure out adrenaline cured the boredom. Around seventeen I started racing cars. Not legally, mind you."

A huff of sarcastic laughter puffed against his chest. "What would be the fun in that?"

"Exactly. The more dangerous, the better. Some of my degenerate friends turned to drugs for adventure and the high, but I never found that satisfying."

"You like to be challenged, not to be out of control."

"Pretty much. Street racing, skydiving, BASE jumping. You name it—if I could get a hit of adrenaline, I was in."

"What does this have to do with Sawyer?" There was the question he'd been expecting.

"Sawyer was the angel to my devil. Studious and serious. While I had no intention of working at the company at all, he always planned to take over. My parents recognized that and began grooming him for the position at an early age."

"Did that bother you? Them choosing him over you?"

"Not at all." Bitter laughter squeezed from his chest. "I felt sorry for Sawyer, although I know he didn't dread the idea of it as I did. The thing was, since our parents were always gone, the two of us pretty much only had each other. We were very close, even though we were very different."

"Not surprising."

"But we also fought. All the time."

"Also not surprising. You were brothers. And young."

"Maybe so. The older I got, the worse it became. Because Sawyer didn't approve of any of the things I enjoyed doing. He was constantly harping on me that I was going to die young."

What irony that Sawyer had been the one to fulfill that prophecy.

Caught up in his own misery and memories, Finn hadn't realized he'd stopped talking until Genevieve asked, "What happened?"

"He followed me to a race one night, pissed that I was going. There was a rumor the police had been tipped off about the intended track, so the location changed at the last minute. Somehow, he got word the new location had been compromised, as well. He followed me to stop me, but I wouldn't listen. We argued, but I got in the car, anyway."

God, he would never forget the utter anger on Sawyer's face as Finn had driven to the starting line and roared away.

"I didn't see the accident. I just heard about it later. The cops did show up. There was a scramble as people left. And somehow, Sawyer was hit. They told me he died on impact."

Finn shrugged, words backing up into a lump in his throat.

"That doesn't change the fact that he's gone." Genevieve's soft voice washed over him.

"No, it doesn't. He shouldn't have been there. It's my fault."

She stirred again, trying to move so she could see him. Finn tightened his arms around her, but this time she wouldn't be put off. Wiggling free, she pushed up so she could look at him.

"You're smarter than that, Finn. You know it's not true."

"Maybe."

Grasping his face, she brought them nose-to-nose. "No. You didn't hit him."

"It should have been me."

"That's not how life works. I lost my parents when I was so young that I don't have a single memory of either of them."

"I wish I didn't have a memory of mine. I identified Sawyer's body. I was nineteen. Our parents let their staff make the arrangements for his funeral. They flew in that morning and flew out again that night. Some business deal in Hong Kong that couldn't be postponed."

"Jesus. My grandfather is a demanding, dictatorial asshole, but your parents might be worse."

Finn shrugged. "They're gone now. Died in a plane crash in Thailand nine months after Sawyer."

Genevieve made a strangled sound in the back of her throat.

"Trust me, it wasn't a loss."

Her eyes were damp. Finn stared at Genevieve, taking in the sadness that filled her. For him. He didn't think anyone had ever cried for him.

"I'm so sorry," she whispered.

"Not your fault."

"No, but that doesn't stop me from caring you've experienced that pain. Thank you."

"For what?"

"Giving me this piece of you."

Dropping back down onto the bed beside him, Genevieve wrapped her arms around him and squeezed. She simply held him, soothing away something that wasn't her fault or responsibility.

Giving him peace he hadn't known he'd desperately needed.

Finn stared at the imposing structure of the museum across the street. The soaring columns were impressive, not to mention the history of the building itself. Once a church used as a hospital during the Civil War, now it housed the largest private collection of historic manuscripts.

Most people would be surprised to discover Finn had an affinity for "old paper." But the documents, manuscripts and scores housed inside the building held history, revolution and humanity. They were the memory of mistakes and triumphs. Lessons the rest of the world needed to remember so as not to repeat.

Not to mention, manuscripts and historical documents could be quite valuable.

But this place had one piece that always held a special place in his heart—the stage version of Twain's *The Adventures of Tom Sawyer.*

Standing out front, it was child's play to catalog the weaknesses in their security. It wouldn't take much effort for him to take ownership of the piece. Only one thing kept him from following through—he appreciated the ideas the museum had been founded on.

Not to mention, he had a hard and fast rule about stealing from nonprofits. Taking something from a private collector who got off on keeping precious works of art hidden behind walls and barriers for the sole purpose of ownership…that was reprehensible.

This was just him getting itchy.

He'd been restless since his conversation with Genevieve. Opening up to her about Sawyer had left him feeling…uncomfortable.

He'd pulled his first job weeks after Sawyer's death. Planning the heist had been a distraction from the grief and guilt. The ultimate high to drown out the pain when it had gone flawlessly and he'd walked away with a priceless work of art.

Standing outside the museum—effortlessly formulating a plan he had no intention of using—was a needed reminder of just who he was.

Someone who would never deserve to be a part of the happy family Genevieve would someday have.

Hell, it had been less than two weeks and he was already straining beneath the mantle of domesticity. Ignoring the urges deep inside him, pretending to be the man she wanted and needed, was exhausting. Not to mention, doomed to failure.

Deep down, he would always be a criminal. Dangerous to those around him that mattered.

Maybe it would be better if he admitted that right now. Reminded them both that he wasn't a good man.

He wasn't who Genevieve wanted him to be.

The rub was, a huge part of him wanted to be who she saw when she looked at him. But Finn had no idea how to do that.

One thing was for certain, walking inside that museum and stealing a historically valuable document simply because it reminded him of his brother wouldn't accomplish anything.

Ten

Finn turned from the museum and headed back to his car, restless energy still humming seductively beneath his skin. Slipping into the soft leather seats, he connected his phone to the Bluetooth and hit one of the few numbers programmed in.

He slammed the gas pedal to the floor and roared out of the parking lot, uncaring for the nasty looks he received on his way out—a guy needed to get thrills where he could—just as the call connected.

"Finn," Stone's dry voice answered.

"I'm itchy as hell and about to do something stupid." That was as close to a cry for help as he was going to get.

"Where are you? I'm coming to you."

This was why Stone was one of his best friends. No

hesitation, question or censure. Just support and immediate action.

"No need. I'm coming to you."

Hitting the button to end the call, Finn let the force of the car push him back into the cradle of the expensive leather seat. His fingers wrapped tightly around the steering wheel, not just gripping for control of the car.

Ten minutes later, he walked in the front door at Stone Surveillance and straight back to Stone's office. Knocking the door closed behind him, he sprawled into the waiting chair across from his friend's glossy desk.

Stone didn't bother to ask questions. He walked to the sideboard, poured two fingers of Scotch into cut-crystal glasses and handed him one. "Talk to me."

Frowning into the amber liquid, Finn stared at it for a few seconds before knocking it back and swallowing it in one gulp. The liquor burned down the back of his throat, but he welcomed the pain of it.

"I can't do it," he finally murmured.

"Do what?"

"Go straight." Finn dropped the glass onto the top of Stone's desk and then stared up at his friend. "It's only been a few weeks and I'm chafing against the perfect family picture Genevieve is painting me into. We both know I'm not a nice guy and I've never professed to be one. Eventually, I'm going to screw up, man."

Stone crossed his arms over his chest, leaned his hips back against the edge of his desk and pulled his lips into a frown. "From everything you've told me and the reports I've read, Genevieve strikes me as a pretty practical woman. Not to mention intelligent."

"She is."

"Something tells me she's perfectly aware of the kind of man you are and doesn't expect you to be anything you're not, including perfect."

"For someone so smart, you can be incredibly stupid" was Finn's dry response.

"Funny, Piper likes to tell me the same thing. I think you're both wrong. But I'm absolutely certain of it where Genevieve is concerned. Have you talked to her about any of this?"

"Hell, no. Given our history, I'm certain the last thing she wants to hear about is my struggle to go straight."

"I don't know. I have a feeling she'd be pretty supportive."

Finn scoffed. "You know nothing about women."

"Bullshit. I'm the only one of us who's currently planning a wedding." Stone waved a hand, cutting off any rebuttal Finn could make. "None of that matters. I have a solution that might get you the adrenaline fix you need in a way that's perfectly legal."

Finn was pretty certain nothing legal could provide him the same challenge or gratification that stealing could.

"Whatever."

"No, seriously. Listen to me."

Finn shrugged. He didn't have much choice. He'd come to Stone, after all.

"Why do you think I've been pressuring you to join the company?"

"Because you're an asshole." And a good friend. "But

you've gotten your way." As usual. "So what does that have to do with anything?"

"I have a client I think you can help."

Finn scoffed. "You have someone who needs a painting stolen?"

"Yes."

"Yeah, right." Stone was as straight a shooter as Finn had ever encountered. He might have spent ten years in prison, but he was hardly a criminal. In fact, the time he did break the law was in defense of his fiancée, killing her rapist. There was no way in hell Stone would agree to take on a client who wanted them to steal something. Stone had too much honor for that.

"Actually, our client already had a priceless artifact stolen from his office."

No doubt the idiot had displayed the piece in an attempt to make himself feel powerful and in control, but failed to protect the item. "I'm going out on a limb to suggest he deserved to lose it."

"Probably."

"So you and Gray are helping to recover the piece." Finn didn't bother to ask the question, he already knew that's what his friends were going to do. Because their sense of honor where this kind of thing was concerned happened to be a bit different from his own.

"Yes."

"Great, you know that's not something I'm going to help with."

"I know."

"Exactly what do you need me for, then?"

"He's also asked us to assess his security around the rest of his personal collection."

"And you want me to point out where his holes are."

"Yes. But I want you to do more than just observe and assess. I want you to break in and steal whatever you can get your hands on."

Finn tipped his head sideways, staring at Stone and trying to figure out if he was being serious. "What does that accomplish? Just assess his system, tell him where the weaknesses are and get him to sign off on the upgrades."

"He wants a more hands-on approach."

Well, bully for him. "People in hell want ice water."

"Let's just say this guy has enough money to purchase your specialized skill set."

"Too bad I don't give a shit how much money he has. I don't need it." Finn lasered Stone a pointed glance. "Neither do you."

His friend shrugged. "True, but Stone Surveillance does need the funds."

"Bullshit."

"How about we need the word of mouth in order to build the business? We're not planning to advertise. We're only looking to take on niche clients."

"Or bleeding-heart stories and clients who need real help." Because that was his friend. Stone had billions of dollars and could spend the rest of his life sitting on the sand somewhere with a cold drink in his hand. But that wasn't Stone.

"We're lucky, Finn. You, me and Gray. We've all had our problems, but at the end of the day our bank accounts afford us access to resources that allow us benefits others don't have."

Apparently, not enough benefits since all three of them had spent plenty of time in prison. Although he had to admit that, out of the three of them, he was the only one who'd actually deserved to be there. Stone had been defending someone he loved from a monster. And Gray... Finn had no doubt Gray was innocent of the charges he'd been convicted of.

And that was a puzzle he'd happily spend the rest of his life helping his friend solve.

But in the meantime... "This client of yours sounds like he has plenty of resources all on his own. Why does he need our help?"

"He's a close family friend. A man I've known my entire life."

"Ahhh." There was the connection.

"And taking paying clients allows us to help the ones who can't afford help on their own. The ones who really need us."

"You're going to keep talking until I agree to do this, aren't you?"

"Remember that agreement you made when you signed the ownership paperwork? Let's consider this your contribution to the company."

"Asshole."

Stone grinned at him. "Do you wanna see the specs on his system or not?"

Finn let out a low growl, but waved his fingers, indicating Stone should bring it on.

"What the hell does this guy own, anyway?"

"One of the largest private art collections in the South. He has several paintings from Rembrandt, Degas, Pollock, van Gogh and Basquiat. He also fancies himself an amateur archaeologist and likes to purchase artifacts from ancient civilizations. He's not selfish, though, and regularly loans his pieces out to museums around the world."

"Jesus," Finn grumbled. "Sounds like a guy with more money than sense."

"No, he's simply a collector who likes to believe he's preserving art and history for the next generations."

"Without spending the time and money he needs to protect that history."

"That's where you come in. He recognizes the need to up his game. And he's willing to invest in the best. Use your expertise. Get up close and personal with his systems. Tell us what he needs so we can help him preserve that culture for others."

Finn didn't like this. Something about it felt wrong, but he also couldn't fault Stone for his argument.

"You've known this guy for a long time?"

"Yes. He's given his permission for us to have unfettered access to whatever we need. And he's aware we might have unconventional methods for assessing his current security."

"Well, that takes all the fun out of things, doesn't it?"

A wicked half smile tugged at Stone's mouth. "Not really. We won't tell him what you're doing. I might be able to get you out of jail after the fact, but if you get caught breaking in, you're likely going to spend some time behind bars again."

"Not to mention give my probation officer heart palpitations."

"So don't get caught."

For the first time since walking into Stone's office, excitement began to bubble through Finn's veins. "Oh, I have no intention of getting caught, my friend."

Genevieve pushed back from the microscope she'd been using to create the setting for the alexandrite necklace. The platinum filigree and brilliance of the tiny diamonds she was using as accents would be a perfect contrast for the deep, rich colors of the bigger stones. Ever since talking with Finn about the pieces a week ago, things had started to fall into place. This felt right, when everything else she'd attempted had felt oh-so-wrong.

Inspiration was a fickle and amazing thing.

It was also an unrelenting taskmaster. She'd spent more hours in the studio over the last week, driven to finish the piece as quickly as possible, than she had in the last month. When she wasn't in the studio, she was cramming in as much time with Finn and Noah as she could.

There was no hiding the fact that she was exhausted. There just weren't enough hours in the day, which made her feel guilty. The only thing that held the guilt at bay right now was the idea that it would all be over in just a few weeks. After that, she was going to take a long break and make it up to her son.

Rubbing at her eyes to try and get them to refocus

after being tunneled down to just the piece, Genevieve let her body sag against the chair.

"You're working too hard."

She jumped, the rolling casters on the bottom of her chair rattling as it moved several inches before being caught and stopped.

Craning her head around, she stared up into Nick's face. "You startled me."

"I'm sorry. I didn't mean to. I was just coming to let you know I'm heading out for the night. And suggest you do the same. You've had your head stuck in that scope for hours."

Shifting his hands, Nick brushed the hair away from her neck and began digging his thumbs into the top of her spine. "Your neck has to be killing you after sitting hunched over like that for so long."

Genevieve didn't realize the ache was even there until he started rubbing. Letting out a deep groan, she sank into the relief his capable hands were giving her.

But after a few minutes, once the initial pain had subsided, a sense of unease trickled through her. Damn Finn and his poisonous thoughts. Nick was a friend and nothing more. He'd rubbed her neck this way before, countless times. In her own studio and when they'd both worked at Reilly.

It meant nothing.

Still, twisting, Genevieve stood up and offered Nick a grateful smile. "Thanks. I didn't realize how tight my muscles were."

"No problem." Taking a step toward the door, Nick

said, "I'm heading out. Why don't you leave, too? I can lock up for you."

Genevieve looked longingly at the door. A part of her wanted to do just that. Go home, scoop her son up into her arms, feed him dinner and give him a bath. Then curl up beside Finn on the couch and neck like teenagers in front of the TV, watching a show neither of them cared anything about.

But there was also a part of her that didn't want to go home. Because home was complicated and uncertain. What the hell was she doing with Finn?

Anyone looking in would say they were in a relationship. A family. But…she wasn't sure that's what was really going on. Or what she wanted.

Could she ever let herself trust Finn again? Or trust herself around him?

Sure, Finn challenged her. He'd been the first person to recognize who she was, and tell her there was nothing wrong with being that person. Even if her grandfather had always told her she was stupid, useless and wrong.

And then, by his actions, Finn had managed to taint the self-discovery that had started to make her feel empowered. Sure, over the last three years she'd found her own inner power, but now that he was back in her life…

Bottom line was, she didn't trust her own instincts around Finn. He clouded her judgment. He made her reckless.

If it was just her, she might enjoy the ride and deal with consequences later. But it wasn't just her. Unfortunately, the same thing that made her cautious was the same thing that would keep Finn in her life for a very long time. It wasn't as simple as trying to resist.

She'd already proven she sucked at resisting Finn DeLuca.

So, giving in to what was between them was inevitable. But she needed to find a way to keep pieces of herself safe and protected, even as he became a bigger part of her life.

"No, I need to get more done."

While that was true, part of her just needed some distance…because after the last couple weeks, all of her defenses were sorely close to crumbling.

Nick left. Alone, Genevieve rolled back to her equipment and began working the delicate filigree. It was intricate work that required her full attention. She had no idea how long she stayed that way, although her shoulders were aching again, when an unexpected sound broke through her concentration.

Pulling back, she listened for it again. It didn't take long to hear a rattle at the back door. Her heart lurched into her throat and she jumped out of her chair, simultaneously grabbing for her phone. Without thinking, she pulled up Finn's number and punched the call button.

What she didn't expect was to hear the echoing sound of his ringtone faintly coming from the other side of her back door just before it opened. If she hadn't heard his phone, she might have screamed. Although most burglars didn't come burdened down with enough bags and boxes that they could barely see over the stack.

"What the hell?" she asked, not sure what she wanted

to know more: why he was there, what he was carrying or what his plan was.

Because there was no question Finn DeLuca was up to something.

Ducking sideways, he flashed her that mischievous, charming smile that always made her knees weak. "I come bearing gifts."

"Obviously. Why?"

"A surprise."

Because suddenly showing up at her studio wasn't surprise enough? "I'm not particularly fond of surprises."

Which wasn't entirely true. But she wasn't exactly a fan of Finn's surprises. So far, not many of them had been happy.

"You'll like this one. I hope."

"Hmm," she hummed, unconvinced.

Kicking the door shut behind him with the heel of a shiny dress shoe, Finn strode across the room and dumped his armful of packages onto an empty worktable.

That's when she realized he was dressed in a tux.

"Hot damn." It was unfair how good the man looked all dressed up. He reminded her of some dashing Victorian duke.

Finn flashed her a knowing grin, smoothed his hands over the sides of his jacket and said, "Glad you approve."

Egotistical ass. The man knew exactly how amazing he looked, which was both charming and frustrating at the same time. "A little overdressed for a night watching TV, don't you think?"

"Probably, so it's a good thing that's not what we're doing."

"Oh, no? I don't know about your plans, but that's exactly how I intended to spend my night. Besides, someone has to get back to our son. The babysitter would probably appreciate going home."

He cut her a wounded look. "What little faith. I've arranged for Maddie to get Noah. He's spending the night with her and excited about the idea, I might add."

Genevieve wasn't sure how that should make her feel, a little excited and sad at the same time apparently. Conflicted, which is how Finn often made her feel.

"All right," she responded, pulling the words into multiple syllables, waiting for the rest of the information. When Finn wasn't forthcoming, she finally asked, "And just why did you go to all the trouble?"

"Because I need to attend a benefit gala tonight and I'd love for you to accompany me."

"A benefit gala?" Dread and irritation mixed in her belly. She'd attended her fair share of fancy events. Been hostess for her grandfather at several. None had ever been a fun experience. She'd rather enjoyed skipping them the last few years. "These kind of things don't just spring up overnight. Why are you telling me about this now?"

"The invitation came in weeks ago, but I wasn't planning to attend."

"What changed?"

He shrugged. "A friend asked me to go."

Grabbing a garment bag from the pile, he spread it

across the table. "Before you protest that you don't have anything to wear, I've obviously taken care of that."

Pulling open the zipper, he revealed a breathtaking emerald green lace gown. Genevieve couldn't help but step closer so she could run her hands over the material. The lace was so intricate and delicate, soft beneath her fingertips.

She had to admit the only benefit to the events had always been getting dressed up. Putting on beautiful clothes had always made her feel elegant and pretty, something that didn't happen often.

Until Finn. He always had the ability to make her feel gorgeous with nothing more than a hot, burning glance.

Reaching inside the bag, Finn lifted the gown out so she could get the full effect. It was strapless with a corset bodice that three years ago would have made her feel naked and inappropriate. But the way Finn was watching her right now made her think he was already imagining her in the dress.

And out of it.

Gesturing to the bags still strewn across her table, Genevieve said, "I hope you had the forethought to bring undergarments."

A wicked grin crinkled the corners of his eyes. Finn tossed the dress onto the table and grasped her instead. Pulling her close, he brushed his lips against the sensitive shell of her outer ear and whispered, "Sweetheart, what makes you think I want you wearing anything beneath this dress?"

Genevieve pulled in a sharp breath, a little because

she was scandalized, but mostly because her body warmed to Finn's outrageous words.

Pulling back, he grabbed the dress, draped it over her arms, spun her around and gave her a gentle shove. "Go put it on."

Genevieve found herself walking across the studio toward the tiny attached bathroom. It wasn't until she'd closed the door and began taking her clothes off that she realized he hadn't actually given her anything to put on underneath.

Eleven

Finn waited impatiently for Genevieve to emerge. She was going to look amazing in the dress. If there was one thing he recognized, it was beauty.

Genevieve Reilly was gorgeous inside and out.

Needing something to keep him busy, Finn started pulling the rest of the things he'd brought from the bags and boxes. Yes, he'd included panties—and made sure they were tiny and lacy—although a huge part of him hoped Genevieve let her inner vixen out and decided not to wear them.

Knowing she was walking around, hobnobbing with the Charleston elite completely naked under the dress he'd bought her…not only would he find that amusing, but he'd most definitely need to find some quiet alcove to pull her into so he could take advantage of her naked state.

He'd brought a couple pairs of shoes, makeup and an assortment of hair products. The last thing he pulled out was the case for the emerald pieces he'd bought. He tucked the box out of sight, wanting to save that surprise for last.

He couldn't wait to see their gorgeous color against her creamy skin. He'd purposely picked out the dress to complement the pieces so that he could show off Genevieve and her skills as an artist.

The door slowly creaked open. Genevieve stood, framed by the doorway, a complete vision. Finn's dick went half-hard and his heart thumped erratically against his chest.

"You're stunning," he whispered.

The answering smile that dawned across her face made his heart kick even harder. *Crap.* He wanted to be the reason for that expression every day for the rest of her life.

And he had no idea what to do with that revelation. "Thanks."

Swiping an arm over the table, he said, "You should have everything you need."

Walking across the room toward him, Finn couldn't help but appreciate the way the dress clung to her luscious curves. He knew there was a fine layer of beige mesh beneath the lace covering her body, but the illusion that she was naked between the intricate work made his brain threaten to explode.

Walking close, Genevieve let her body brush against

his. She watched his reaction from beneath her lashes, the little vixen.

His straitlaced rule follower was feeling a little wild. And he was happy to encourage that kind of behavior.

Wrapping an arm around her waist, Finn pulled her tight against his body. He strategically placed her so the edge of her hip rubbed right against the erect ridge pushing against the constricting teeth of his zipper.

Finding her ear, he murmured, "Yes, there are panties somewhere in this pile. My question is, are you brave enough to leave them here?"

Shaking her head, Genevieve stretched out, rummaging through everything until she found the panties he'd bought. Just like the dress, they were a deep emerald green, silk and lace.

Fingers tucked inside the waistband, she pulled until they went taught and then flipped them around so she could see the tiny string that constituted the back. Pursing her lips, she turned her head and looked him straight-on.

He expected to get a lecture on how inappropriate they were. So he was surprised when, instead, Genevieve neatly folded them into a little fan, yanked out the square of material tucked into the pocket of his jacket and replaced it with the panties she obviously wouldn't be wearing.

God, this woman was amazing. A constant surprise.

"You're trying to kill me, aren't you?"

"Nope, that would be stupid. I really want you to make love to me later. Hard to do if you're dead."

What he wanted to do was shove the skirt of her

dress up and sink into her body right now. But if he did that, they'd never make it to the gala. And he really needed to be there tonight.

The gala was being held at Dennis Hunt's home. Hunt happened to be Stone's client. This was the perfect opportunity to survey the estate, review the security measures and find some vulnerabilities.

Seeing Genevieve all dressed up was simply the cherry on top of the sundae.

"As much as I'd like to show you that playing with fire gets you burned, we don't have time. The car will be here in twenty minutes." Sweeping a hand over the table, he continued. "You're perfect just the way you are, but if you want makeup and hair now's the time."

Genevieve quickly picked through the products, gathering a few in her hands. Tossing a saucy smile over her shoulder, she headed back to the bathroom.

This time she didn't bother shutting the door. So Finn followed, leaning a shoulder against the jamb so he could watch. With a few sure strokes, she applied just enough makeup to highlight her face. Then with nothing more than a band, some pins and a curling wand, she managed to put her hair up in some elegant twist that made her look both sexy and sophisticated.

Less than fifteen minutes later, she was shooing him out of the doorway so she could pick out a pair of heels. He'd brought several options, not just so she could have color choices, but because he wasn't certain what heel height she'd be most comfortable wearing.

He was slightly surprised when she picked out a pair of strappy sandals about four inches high. But he was grateful when she walked across the room in them, her hips swaying seductively.

Reaching behind him, Finn pulled out the case he'd stashed. Genevieve faltered, her steps stuttering in a way that had him extending his arm to her because he was afraid she was falling.

But she wasn't. She was solid on her feet, her eyes trained on the box in his hand.

Nerves suddenly fluttered deep in his belly. Finn couldn't remember the last time he'd been nervous about anything.

Opening the lid, he held the jewels out to her.

"I wanted you to wear these."

Her eyes drifted across the pieces nestled against the black velvet inside. Pride, peace and happiness flitted across her face.

But she didn't move to touch them.

Dropping the box onto the table, Finn lifted out the necklace. It was light and cool against his hands, just as it would be until the heat of her body warmed it.

Stepping up to her, he waited until she spun so he could place the necklace around her neck. The teardrop settled into the valley at the center of her throat. It moved as she swallowed.

The backs of Finn's fingertips brushed across her soft skin. Genevieve shivered. Following the line, he worked the clasp and then reluctantly dropped his hands away.

And waited for her to spin around.

He wasn't disappointed with the vision she made when she did. But he didn't speak. Not yet. Reaching back into the box, he pulled out the set of earrings, handing them to her one at a time as she leaned sideways to put them in. The matching bracelet followed.

Only then did he take a step back so that he could appreciate the full impact of her.

"You are beautiful every minute of every day, but right now...you glow. The jewels around your neck pale in comparison to your fire and light."

Genevieve's eyes sparkled and shimmered. For a moment he was worried she might start crying, but instead a radiant smile curled her lips. Closing the gap between them, she placed both of her palms against his chest and leaned close.

"You make me feel beautiful, Finn. And you always have. You've always been happy to share your own intense fire and excitement for life." Touching her mouth to his, she whispered, "Thank you."

Finn wasn't certain if she was thanking him for tonight or for something else, but it really didn't matter.

He was just about to say to hell with the gala, he'd find another way to survey Hunt's estate, when his cell buzzed letting him know the car had arrived.

"Perfect timing," he mumbled irritably, before sweeping a hand toward the back door. "After you."

Genevieve was familiar with the world she'd just entered. It had simply been a long time since she'd been back.

The imposing brick mansion, lights blazing out over a forecourt lined with towering oaks, didn't impress her. It did remind her of movies like *Gone with the Wind* and *Midnight in the Garden of Good and Evil*, though.

Uniformed employees opened the doors as they approached, revealing a sweeping double staircase framing the entrance to a ballroom filled with elegantly clad people. Everything sparkled and shimmered, especially the women milling about.

This was definitely something she hadn't missed for the past few years. These kinds of events had been regular affairs in her life with her grandfather. She was expected to be the perfect companion, quiet and unimposing. Demure and obedient. An example he could point to when he wanted to praise his own parenting skills and a disappointment and burden he could reference when he wanted to play the martyr.

She'd hated every minute, usually finding the events boring and tedious.

Something told her tonight would be much different.

Proving her point, the material of her dress brushed against the naked mound of her sex, sending a thrill racing through her blood. Finn didn't help matters any when he let his hand drop from the dip of her hip to the rounded flesh of her rear…and gave her a hard squeeze.

Elbowing him in the side, Genevieve cut him a disapproving glance. His response was an impish grin that suggested he planned to ignore her hint.

Letting his hand slide into hers, Finn led her to the heart of the ballroom, sweeping past people, uncaring when they attempted to stop him and speak.

Genevieve had no doubt one of the things that drew people to Finn was his complete lack of caring about what others thought…or wanted. At least generally speaking. If someone wasn't important to him, their opinion or needs mattered not at all.

That attitude came with an air of confidence that was attractive and seductive. She'd seen the phenomenon before. People were drawn to Finn. And it was no less true tonight.

Of course, it didn't hurt that he had a reputation for being outrageous and an air of danger because of his history. People delighted in gossiping behind his back, but wanted to be able to say they knew him for the shock value it could provide.

Finn didn't give a rip about any of it.

Over the next thirty minutes or so Finn kept a tight arm around her shoulders or waist, ensuring she stayed close. He spoke to a handful of people, carrying on banal conversations that he was very careful to be sure included her.

He made it clear—to her if not to anyone else—with his actions and words that as far as he was concerned, she was the most important person in the room.

Which eventually had a flock of women surrounding her as they attempted to figure out how she fit into things. Several of them she'd been acquainted with through her grandfather and her work at Reilly, although none were what she'd consider friends.

Needing a break, she was about to excuse herself and find a ladies' room where she could hide for a few minutes when she registered a change in Finn's tone of voice. Before, his words had held a clipped, bored undertone. Now, whoever he spoke with actually mattered.

Genevieve turned her attention back to Finn, closing the small gap that had developed as they engaged with different conversations. Coming up beside him, she realized a gorgeous couple stood across from him.

What struck her immediately as she slipped her hand into his was how relaxed his body was. Until that moment, she hadn't realized the thin layer of tension snapping through him. His expression now was free and easy. Comfortable.

She'd seen Finn interact with many people—tonight and several years ago. He was always in complete control, of himself, of the situation and of the people around him. But in order to be that way, he had to constantly be on.

With the couple in front of him, she realized he didn't feel that need. Which intrigued her.

Turning her attention to them, Genevieve immediately began cataloging them both. The man was a couple inches over six feet. Just like Finn, he was obviously fit beneath the layers of polish and expensive clothing. His facial features were sharp, and not simply because he had an aristocratic heritage. His personality and demeanor added even more of an edge. Without the smile on his lips and the crinkled edges at his eyes he could have been austere and intimidating.

Genevieve had no doubt there were times that's exactly how he came across. Because he could be when necessary.

But not with Finn.

The woman standing beside him was stunning in a girl-next-door way. Tonight she was wearing a couture gown that was simple even as it showed off her petite

frame. She didn't need beads, sequins or crystals because they would have appeared garish next to her elegant beauty. Her blond hair was pulled back into a
demure knot at the base of her head. She could have
come across as aloof and snobbish, except that her eyes
glowed with joy and genuine interest.

Separately they would have been intimidating. Together, their love for each other was so obvious that
you couldn't help but want to bask in their happiness
so some of it could rub off.

Genevieve was about to introduce herself so she
could learn who they were to Finn, but he beat her to it.

Wrapping an arm around her waist, he pulled Genevieve against his side.

"Genevieve, let me introduce you to Stone and Piper,
two of my closest friends."

By his own admission Finn allowed few people close
enough to call friends. So it was easy to make assump-
tions about who Stone was. Not that she'd needed the
deduction once she'd heard their names.

Anderson Stone and Piper Blackburn had been in the
news several months ago. Genevieve might not know
the intimate details of their situation, but she understood enough.

Holding out a hand, she said, "Wonderful to meet
you both."

Stone accepted her offering, giving her hand a
squeeze. Piper, though, didn't bother. She moved
straight past Genevieve's outstretched hand to pull her
close and wrap her in a tight hug. Pulling back, she gave
Genevieve a brilliant smile. "We need to get together

for drinks and dinner soon. I want to get to know you better."

In that moment, Genevieve decided that she really liked Piper. "That would be great."

Piper drew her a few steps away from the men, sharing a little about herself and asking questions of her own.

"How's your son?"

At first Genevieve was taken aback that the other woman seemed to know more about her than a stranger normally would. Until she continued.

"I've seen pictures. He's adorable, by the way. And heard plenty of stories. Noah is one of Finn's favorite topics. He's such a proud daddy."

Placing a hand on Genevieve's arm, Piper leaned closer. "I know it's none of my business, but I just want to say that from a professional standpoint, I admire your ability to separate your personal issues with Finn and let him be a father to Noah. I have plenty of patients still dealing with the aftermath of an absent father."

Genevieve blinked, uncertain how to respond.

Piper pulled a grimace. "I'm sorry. Stone's always telling me I need to keep my psychologist firmly locked away during these events. I just know it couldn't have been easy at first to let Finn back into your life given the history between you. I'm impressed. And it says a lot about you as a person and a mom."

Well, okay. "Thanks?" Was that the proper response when someone praised you for being a decent human being? "I admit I wasn't thrilled and tried to stop Finn from being involved at first. But once I had no choice…

finding a way to interact became important for Noah's happiness. And the first time I saw Finn with him..."

How could she not have allowed him into Noah's life? No matter what else happened, Genevieve knew Finn loved their son and would do anything to protect him.

That was all she could ask of him.

Waving a hand to change the subject, Piper said, "No more of that. Finn said you're a jewelry designer. Did you make the pieces you're wearing?"

"Yes."

"They're stunning."

"Thank you. Finn bought them from one of my consignment clients."

Genevieve couldn't stop her gaze from dragging across the space to find him. At some point he and Stone had moved several more feet away. At the edge of the room, they were standing half in shadows, heads bowed together in conversation.

Finn was relaxed. Stone, on the other hand, was frustrated and irritated. Leaning into Finn's personal space, he was attempting to make a point with whatever words he was using. While Finn was clearly unswayed.

"What are they talking about?" she found herself asking Piper.

The other woman shrugged. "Who knows. Those two are the best of friends, but Finn delights in irritating Stone. I'm pretty sure it's a game to him. One I keep pointing out to Stone that he's letting Finn win."

Piper shifted, turning her back to the men again. Genevieve couldn't pull her gaze away from them, though. Something about the conversation made her uneasy. To anyone else watching, Finn most likely appeared to be unaffected by what his friend was saying. But Genevieve knew him better than most.

He was upset.

"I wish Gray was here. He's usually the peacemaker between them. I've learned from experience not to get between them when they get going. It doesn't do much good."

"Gray?"

"The third member in their little trio. All three met in prison, but I assume you already knew that."

Genevieve nodded.

"Gray was convicted of embezzling forty million, although all three of the guys contend he was framed. They've been working together for months to try and find proof to back up their claim."

"Any luck?"

"Not so far."

"Because there isn't any evidence or because they haven't been able to find it?"

Piper's gaze cut to hers. Her head tilted sideways as she studied Genevieve for several moments. Genevieve fought the urge to squirm beneath the sharp, intelligent, all-too-seeing gaze.

After several seconds, she finally said, "My money's on they just haven't been able to find it. Yet. Everyone in prison claims to be innocent...except Stone and Finn. They both readily admitted to doing what they were convicted of. Gray's always maintained his innocence."

Twelve

"You brought her with you to rob the place?" Stone asked, a frown pulling his brows into an unhappy V.

"No, I brought her to a benefit gala for a charity I'm happy to support."

"Bullshit."

Finn shrugged his shoulders. "You asked me to take on this project. Let me do it."

"Oh, I have no qualms with your ability to successfully complete the assignment. I do, however, question your judgment in bringing Genevieve into it."

"Really? She's the perfect cover for a little theft."

"Sure. Until she figures out you've used her and then she's gonna be pissed."

"She'll never know."

"Uh-huh. Man, if there's one thing I've learned it's

that women always find out." Stone sent a sardonic expression in Piper's direction. If Finn was a better friend, he might ask questions about what Stone was talking about.

But he wasn't a good friend.

Finn shrugged. "I'll take my chances."

"You'll have a preliminary report tomorrow?"

Business concluded, Finn was eager to get back to Genevieve. He wanted to enjoy the party for a little while longer before using the cover of the crowd to slip off and see what he could haul home with him.

Returning to the women, the four of them chatted for several minutes. Piper invited Genevieve out for lunch next week and he was happy when she agreed. Lackland had isolated her so much that she'd never really had the opportunity to build strong friendships.

Piper was the kind of woman who liked to take on the wounded and lost. While Genevieve didn't quite fit into that category, he had no doubt Piper would sense her need for friendship and attempt to fill the role. If for no other reason than she liked him and Genevieve was important to him.

Leaning into her personal space, Finn drew her close. "Dance with me," he murmured against her temple.

Her answering nod was slow and deliberate. Leading them out onto the floor, Finn spun her around and into his arms.

Together, they moved with smooth, sure steps. The melody of the music pulsed beneath the surface of his skin. Finn relished the brush of her body against his. The delicate feel of her. The rough brush of lace as his palm slid across her hip. The heat of her melting deep into his blood.

Finn closed his eyes, soaking up each moment.

Which was why he missed the sneak attack.

"I'll have to speak to Hunt about his guest list. Obviously, he doesn't realize that he's let the serpent into the garden."

His arms wrapped around her, Finn couldn't miss the way Genevieve's body stiffened. She couldn't even see the man standing behind her, but it didn't matter. The voice was obviously enough.

Finn tightened his grip on her, maneuvering them both so he could tuck her protectively against his side.

"Grandfather," Genevieve finally spoke, her voice cool and remote.

"Granddaughter," Lackland countered, his snide voice full of disdain. "I see you haven't gotten any smarter. I can't imagine why you'd let this man anywhere near you given what he did the last time you spread your thighs wide."

Finn took a menacing step forward. Lackland didn't flinch. In fact, he moved closer, raising his chin in a taunting invitation to make a spectacle in the middle of the crowded ballroom.

Genevieve was the one who stopped Finn. A cool hand on his arm, she squeezed. "He isn't worth it."

Finn's gaze was hot when he turned to look at her. Her face was pale and drawn, her jaw tight from grinding her teeth.

"Maybe not, but you are and I won't have him making malicious remarks about you."

"Nothing malicious about my remark, DeLuca. You seduced an innocent woman to gain access to my family vault, stole from us and then left my granddaughter alone and pregnant."

"Every sin you just named was mine, not hers."

"She let you do it. I raised her to be smarter than that."

"You raised her to be an obedient servant. But she isn't. She's a human being with feelings and needs."

"And you had no problem exploiting those needs."

Seriously, if Lackland didn't get out of his sight, Finn was going to deck the man. Spectacle be damned. "You better watch your words, old man. Speak that way about her again and you'll regret it."

"The only thing I regret is that you didn't spend more time behind bars. But I'm certain you'll land yourself back there soon enough. A leopard doesn't change its spots."

Finn balled his hand into a fist. Genevieve yanked hard on his arm. "Walk away, Finn. He's goading you into making a scene."

Logically, he knew Genevieve was right. But he wasn't certain it made a difference. Someone needed to put the bully in his place and Finn had been itching to do it for a very long time. If they'd been anywhere else, he wouldn't have hesitated.

But he still had a job to do.

"Fine," he ground out. Turning to Genevieve, he cupped her face in his hands and brought her close enough that he could stare straight into her eyes. "You and Noah do not need this man in your life. He's poison and has nothing to offer anyone. You, on the other hand, are one of the kindest, most talented and beautiful people I've ever met. I have no idea how you managed to flourish when this man did everything in his power to snuff out your light, but I'm grateful that you did."

Genevieve's eyes widened and her mouth opened and closed. He didn't wait for her response, mostly because he didn't want one. What he'd wanted to do was replace her grandfather's toxic words with something more uplifting.

Arm around her waist, Finn turned his back on her grandfather and led them both across the ballroom and into a hallway off the far side.

The first few rooms had blazing lights and knots of people inside. A game room, a drawing room. What he wanted was a few quiet minutes with her.

Farther down the hall, the noise of the party faded. The bright lights were replaced with muted lamps and sconces. Peeking into a room to the left, Finn found a sunroom. Another door down was an office with an imposing desk and a tufted leather sofa.

He made a mental note to come back in a bit, assuming this was the perfect place to hide a safe.

Another two doors down revealed a smaller, intimate room. The far wall was floor-to-ceiling windows that looked out over the rolling lawn of the estate. The other three walls contained soaring shelves of books with several groupings of furniture clearly designed to curl up and relax.

Tugging on her hand, Finn pulled Genevieve inside and shut the door behind them. This was perfect.

A few feet in, she pulled to a stop. "We shouldn't be here."

"Yes, we should."

"No."

Finn reeled her in, using his hold on her hand to draw her to him. So small, she settled into the shelter of his body. Even reluctant, she didn't hesitate to let herself relax against him.

Her trust was a gift, one he never wanted to screw up again.

Bending his knees, Finn brought his mouth to the naked line of her shoulder. Placing gentle kisses along her skin, he followed the curve up to that sensitive spot on the side of her neck.

The sharp inhale of her breath when he nipped right there sent a surge of need thundering through him. The erection he'd been fighting since she walked out of that bathroom came back full force.

Genevieve's fingers, buried beneath his suit jacket at his hips, curled into his body. Her head dropped sideways, giving him better access to tease her with his mouth.

Finn wasn't the kind of guy to let an invitation like that go unaccepted.

Walking backward, he pulled them both farther into the room until a patch of moonlight, streaming through the gigantic windows, fell across Genevieve's pale skin.

Dropping to his knees at her feet, Finn looked up at her. She was gorgeous, but what sent his heart fluttering was the unguarded way she watched him, her eyes filled with hope and something deeper.

Hands braced on his shoulders, she waited.

Slowly, Finn began to gather the hem of her dress in his hands, revealing her ankles, calves and thighs.

But the real jewel was the dark apex of her sex.

"Lean back and grab the table behind you," Finn ordered. He didn't wait for Genevieve to comply before moving in, murmuring, "I've wanted to do this since you stuffed those panties in my pocket."

Spreading the lips of her sex wide, Finn found her warm center glistening with the evidence of her desire. Genevieve's body rocked backward when his mouth latched on to her. Licking, sucking, using every part of his mouth, Finn relished the explosion of her taste across his tongue. The muffled sound of her whimper as she tried to be quiet.

Her hips moved in time with his motions, rocking harder against his mouth, trying to find more. But he wasn't ready to let her go.

Finn kept her teetering on the edge of release, bringing her close and then moving back. He relished the way her wild hands found his hair, tangling in the strands and using the hold to try and get what she wanted.

"Finn," she finally breathed. "Please."

He couldn't deny her anything.

Adding a finger deep inside her body, Finn ran the flat of his tongue across her clit several times. Adding a second finger, he pulsed them in and out, finding the spot that had her whimpering.

Her body drew tight right before the explosion of her orgasm erupted around him. Finn rode it out, milking her body for every speck of pleasure she could give him.

But the moment she went lax, he shot to his feet and began undoing the fly at his pants. His cock pulsed with the need to feel her warm, wet heat. He wanted to be buried inside her. As close as he could possibly get to her.

Picking her up, Finn flicked the tail of Genevieve's gown out behind her as he set her onto the surface of the table. She hissed at the unexpected cold, but didn't stop him. Instead, she took up the task of freeing him.

Her palm was hot as she stroked up and down his throbbing shaft. "I'm not going to last long if you keep doing that," he breathed.

"Who said anything about lasting long?"

She scooted to the edge of the table. Spreading her thighs wide, Genevieve drew him closer to the waiting heaven she was offering.

Finn bit back a belly-deep groan when he sank inside. She was so wet and warm. Her body fit his like a glove, opening up and welcoming him home. Every time he touched her, he wanted more. Tonight, the need for release was pounding against his brain, but he would have been just as content to stay like this, connected to her in the most primitive and fulfilling way.

But she had other plans.

Hands on his waist, she started guiding him in and out. Finn let her set the pace…for a minute or two. But then it became too much.

Using his grip on her hips, Finn held her steady as he began to pump in and out. Long, even strokes that made his eyes want to cross.

"So damn good," he whispered.

Urging her backward, Finn placed his hands on the tabletop. His thrusts became harder, a rhythmic snap accompanying each as the table tapped the wall behind them.

"Someone's going to hear," Genevieve protested.

"Let them. I want everyone in that ballroom to know you're mine."

Genevieve's eyes sharpened and glittered like the jewels circling her throat. Dropping her head, she exposed the tender underside of her jaw. Finn leaned forward, finding the pulsing vein running along the side and sucked hard.

Her body bowed up and her gasp echoed through the room. Her sex fluttered and tightened around him, another orgasm slamming into her.

And that was all it took for him to topple over. The explosion of pleasure rocked through him, blacking out everything except her.

He was breathing hard several minutes later when his brain clicked back on and everything came into focus. Genevieve had collapsed onto the table beneath him, but she was staring up at him with a sleepy, satisfied expression.

Her hair was messy and her necklace was twisted sideways.

"You look like you just had sex."

A wry grimace pulled at her mouth. "Go figure."

Pulling away, Finn grasped her hands to pull her up. "I've already said it, I don't care what anyone else thinks of us. And I don't mind them knowing we just had sex. But I know you do. So, stay here. I'll go find something to clean us both up."

Quickly working the fly of his pants, Finn strode out into the hallway, but didn't get very far.

His feet faltered halfway past the doorway to the office. It would only take a few moments to do a little reconnaissance.

Genevieve would never know.

Genevieve had no idea how long she stayed in the room. It probably wasn't more than five minutes, but it felt like forever. She was rumpled and clearly sexed up. If anyone walked in right now...

Looking around, Genevieve was hoping to find a mirror hanging on one of the walls that she could at least use to repair her hair. No such luck.

A few more minutes had an anxious sensation pulling at the muscles between her shoulder blades. Maybe Finn had been caught by someone in the hallway and he was attempting to extricate himself from a conversation so he could return to her.

Either way, she was tired of waiting. Surely there was a bathroom somewhere close.

Returning to the hallway, she began moving down, peeking into each room she passed. One door was partially closed so she started to ignore it, but halfway past a noise from the inside caught her attention.

Something made her turn. When she pushed against the door, it didn't even creak as the well-oiled hinges gave way, revealing a large room with an imposing desk prominently displayed.

The piece was massive and intricate. She didn't have to touch it to know it would be heavy. The wood gleamed with the patina of age and the color reminded her of the tobacco leaves she'd once seen on a documentary about Southern plantations.

This room didn't benefit from a massive wall of windows overlooking the back of the estate. The natural light from the few high panes of glass weren't enough to beat back the gloom of darkness that shrouded the edges of the room.

She wasn't supposed to be there.

Genevieve might have backed out, except a movement off to her right caught the corner of her eye. It took her several seconds to register the shape of a man in the shadows, but the minute her eyes picked out the image, the hair at the back of her neck stood on edge.

And not because she was scared.

She didn't need to see clearly to recognize Finn. She'd know the lithe, controlled way he moved anywhere.

Genevieve watched him as he ran his hands along the large frame of a painting mounted on the wall. When that one revealed nothing, he moved to another. The muffled sound of triumph that fell from his lips as he found the catch made her throat ache. The frame swung away from the wall revealing the huge face of an inset safe.

Finn didn't hesitate, but quickly pulled a set of tools out of the pocket of his jacket. How the hell had she missed those? She'd had her hands all over him tonight and hadn't felt them.

He'd brought her here for cover.

Hell, sneaking off to have sex with her had no doubt been another layer to that subterfuge.

He'd used her. And she'd blindly let him.

But she was done accepting that kind of behavior—from him and herself.

The plush carpet silenced her heels as she crossed the room. But something must have tipped him off because he spun around just steps before she could reach him.

"Genevieve," he said, the single word as grim as his expression.

His gaze skipped up and down her body, settling squarely on her face. No doubt she looked like she was pissed. Because she was.

"This isn't what it looks like."

"Oh, you didn't use me so you could break into Hunt's estate and rob him blind?"

"No."

"Bullshit."

"I mean, yes, I am here to rob him, but you weren't cover for that."

Genevieve's head threatened to explode. "I wasn't cover? So I'm just an accomplice instead? Sure, much better. This way our son can lose both his parents when they go to jail."

"Neither one of us is going to jail."

"Because you're going to put—" Genevieve waved her hand toward the tools still clutched in his hands "—whatever those are away, lock the painting back over that safe and we're going to walk out of this room together."

The expression on Finn's face went even grimmer. "I can't do that."

"Oh, yes, you can. If you want to be part of my life, you can."

Closing his eyes, Finn pulled in a deep breath, held it for several seconds and then let out a soul-deep sigh.

"I'm working for Stone."

Seriously, he kept saying things like the words were supposed to make things better, but they just didn't. "I don't care if the queen of England hired you to rob Hunt blind. I won't let you do it."

"The queen of England didn't hire me to rob him, but Hunt did."

Genevieve blinked once. And then again. "Excuse me?"

"Well, technically, he hired Stone Surveillance, but since I'm one-third owner and the resident expert on relieving people of their unprotected valuables, this assignment fell to me."

Seriously. "Are you speaking English?"

"Apparently, Hunt isn't just a longtime friend of your grandfather's. He's known Stone all of his life and been in business with Anderson Steel for years. He approached Stone about beefing up his security, but when Stone made several suggestions, he didn't see the value. They made an agreement, allowing me to break in to take whatever I could."

Genevieve's mind spun with the information. "Why didn't you tell me you'd taken an assignment with Stone? Or that you're part owner in the company?"

"Because until a few days ago I wasn't. Stone's been

trying for months to get me to join the team, but I really didn't want to do it."

"Why not?"

"Because I thought it would be boring. I already own a company and don't enjoy being involved with it. Why would I want to take on the responsibility of another? Especially one that needs to be built from the ground up?"

After meeting him, something told her Anderson Stone would have no problems building the business into whatever he wanted it to become.

"What changed?"

"You did."

For the second time tonight Genevieve found herself asking, "Excuse me?"

"I needed Gray's expertise and Stone's resources in order to get the security at your studio and house upgraded quickly. Stone drives a hard bargain."

"You agreed to something you didn't want to do, something you've been telling your closest friends no about for months, in order to protect me and our son?"

"Of course."

How could she go from wanting to strangle the man to wanting to jump his bones in the space of five minutes? One thing was for sure, Finn DeLuca definitely made her react.

But he wasn't finished shocking her.

"I had every intention of just being a silent partner, in name only." Suddenly, Finn shifted, running an agitated hand through his hair. For the first time since she'd caught him, he began to look guilty. "I'll be honest, I've

loved spending the last few weeks with you and Noah.
But I was starting to get restless, chafe at the normal. I
went to talk to Stone and he suggested I take this job.
Use my skills in a way that might scratch the itch without jeopardizing everything."

Genevieve watched him, trepidation churning sickly
through her belly. She *had* to ask the question, but she
really wasn't sure she wanted to know the answer.

"And?"

A smile tugged at the edges of his mouth. "I thought
knowing it was legit would take the edge off, but it
didn't. Or at least, there was enough left to make the
experience an interesting challenge."

That's what Finn needed and why he did the things
he did. Not because he wanted the things he stole. But
because he wanted to feel alive. Needed to feel alive.

In a way that wouldn't cost someone else their life,
like Sawyer.

God, what was she going to do with him?

Shaking her head, Genevieve was at a loss. She believed him. Maybe she was stupid to, but she did.

Before she could regret it, she grumbled, "Hurry up.
I have your come dripping down my thighs and would
really like to go home."

The shocked laughter that burst from Finn was totally worth it.

Thirteen

The last few days had been a whirlwind of activity. Genevieve had been in the studio all hours of the day and night working on the finishing touches of her collection. Finn had taken to staying at her place, spending time with Noah so she could do what she needed. Aside from playing with his son, the best part of his day was when Genevieve walked through the back door.

He'd finished up his work for Hunt, submitted his report and eventually returned the items he'd taken from the safe. It had actually been more gratifying than he'd anticipated to help design the system and protocols Stone and Gray were implementing to protect the estate.

Tonight, he'd convinced Genevieve that she needed a break. He'd pressured her to leave the studio early.

After running by to see Stone, he'd stopped by his place to pick up a few things.

Finn wondered how long it would be before he could convince Genevieve to move in with him. Her place was nice enough, but it was small. His had more room, although he'd need her help to baby-proof it for sure.

He was halfway back to Genevieve's when an alert went off on his phone. He pulled over to the side of the road, looked at the screen and swore beneath his breath.

An alarm was going off at her studio.

Swiping to open the app, Finn pulled up the video feed. Flipping through the cameras, it took him several minutes to find the shadowy figure creeping through the office and into Genevieve's work area.

No doubt Stone was on it, but he punched in his friend's number, anyway.

Stone didn't bother with a greeting when he answered. "Yeah, man. I see it."

"I'm three minutes away," Finn answered, pulling a U-turn in the middle of the road and heading back in that direction. "I can get there faster than anyone else."

Stone's voice was grim when he said, "I'm calling in reinforcements."

"Thanks," Finn responded, ending the call and tossing his phone onto the seat beside him. He wasn't going to call Genevieve until he knew exactly what they were dealing with. No reason to upset her just yet.

Rushing into the back lot, he parked sideways in front of the back door.

"Dammit," he muttered when he realized it was hanging open several inches.

He was not going to let this happen. Genevieve had worked too hard.

But he also didn't want to alert whoever was inside that they'd been caught. Easing the door open, he slipped inside the studio. The place was pitch-black so he stood for several seconds, letting his eyes adjust to the darkness.

It was difficult to wait, especially when he heard a loud scrape of metal against metal coming from deep inside Genevieve's workroom.

Dread and white-hot anger curled through his stomach.

Slipping into the room, he expected to find some asshole standing in front of the open safe, rummaging through the drawers of jewels.

He was partially right. The doors to Genevieve's vault hung wide open. Several of the drawers were pulled out. But they weren't empty. Pieces spilled haphazardly over the lip of the drawers. A few jewels winked from the floor, scattered like a rainbow crumb trail across the room toward the front door.

Maybe he hadn't been as quiet as he'd thought and had startled the thief.

The good news was several of Genevieve's pieces were still there. The bad news was that the few jewels on the floor were by themselves, which meant they'd been broken apart from the rest of the design.

A string of curse words blasted across Finn's brain.

Torn between wanting to catch whoever was ransacking Genevieve's hard work and not wanting to let something valuable sit vulnerable on the floor, Finn dashed across the room.

But he scooped up the pieces on the floor as he went, stuffing them into the pockets of his slacks.

Bursting into the front room, the sound of sirens in the distance finally registered. Stone must have called the police along with the private team he employed.

He hated that Genevieve was about to spend her night talking with officers. Again. But that process would be easier and better if he could hand them a suspect.

Unfortunately, when Finn reached the front room, no one was there and the door leading onto the sidewalk was standing wide open.

A handful of police cruisers peeled up to the front of the building at the same time he raced out onto the sidewalk. Red-and-blue lights flashed right in his face, making him squint. Finn spun, first to the left and then to the right. The asshole couldn't have gotten far.

But no one was there.

"On the ground," one of the officers shouted.

Finn turned his attention back to the front of the store. Four or five cars were parked in an arch around the building, blocking off the street. A handful of cops had positioned themselves behind the open doors, guns drawn and pointed straight at him.

Well, that was enough to give any man pause.

"On the ground," one of the officers shouted again.

Realizing he didn't have much choice until he could explain the situation, Finn slowly raised his hands up over his head. Folding, he knelt onto the sidewalk.

"Let me explain."

One of the cops holstered his weapon and walked behind him. "You'll have plenty of time to explain."

Finn ignored what they were doing as the officer grabbed his wrists, pulling them behind his back. His words were fast, trying to talk before the cuffs came out.

"The thief is getting away. I work for Stone Surveillance. We got an alert on our security system for Genevieve's Designs. I was close so came to investigate. The back door was wide open. I chased someone through the building, but they slipped out the front door before I could catch them."

Cold metal kissed his skin. The snap around his wrists was a sensation he'd promised himself he'd never experience again.

"The only person we saw in front of the building was you."

Finn turned his head, looking again in both directions. He didn't understand and couldn't explain how that was true. The thief couldn't have moved that quickly. How had they just disappeared?

Urging him up onto his feet, the officer led him over to one of the cruisers. "I'm going to search you now. Anything I need to know about? Weapons? Needles? Anything sharp?"

What the hell did the man take him for? "No. I did scoop up some of the jewels the thief had scattered across the floor. They're in my pockets."

A skeptical expression crossed the officer's face. "Jewels, huh?"

"Look, I knew they weren't safe just sitting on the floor. I needed to secure them."

"Sure, you were just securing them."

Frustration bubbled through him, eating at his patience like battery acid. "Call Anderson Stone. He'll corroborate my story."

"Oh, I'm certain he would. Being a convicted murderer."

"He killed his fiancée's rapist," Finn growled.

The cop shrugged. "Doesn't change the facts. But if what you say is true, we'll sort things out soon enough. Until then, you're being detained for questioning."

How had the night gone so terribly sideways?

He'd planned to spend it at home with Genevieve and Noah. Listening to the belly-deep giggle his son made when he tickled him. Watching the light in Genevieve's eyes when she looked at Noah. Making love to her until they were both exhausted.

Instead, he found himself ducking into the back of a cruiser for the second time in his life.

The worst part was looking through the chaos to find Genevieve standing on the sidewalk, once again watching him as he was carted away.

Pain and devastation stamped across every feature of her face.

How could this be happening again?

Genevieve watched as the officer pulled several gems out of Finn's pockets and placed them inside an evidence bag. She'd gotten a call from Nick saying an alert had come up on the security system.

In between loading up Noah, she'd desperately tried

to get in touch with Finn. But he hadn't answered any of her calls.

Now she understood why.

Scenes from the last several weeks flashed through her mind. Conversations they'd had. Moments they'd shared.

Pain and hope twisted inside her. This couldn't be right. She didn't want to believe he could have done this. There had to be another explanation.

Like at Hunt's.

But the evidence before her was hard to refute.

A huge part of her wanted to trust. Wanted to believe, like with the Star, that there was more to what was going on than met the eye.

Although one irrefutable fact about the Star was that he *had* stolen it. By his own admission he'd had it several days before returning it.

She didn't trust her own judgment when it came to Finn DeLuca. Was she clinging to hope simply because she wanted to? Was she being blind and stupid, ignoring the evidence in front of her?

Watching the officer duck Finn's head down so he could be loaded into the back of the cruiser didn't help at all. In fact, it made her sick to her stomach.

The officer obviously thought there was enough evidence to take him in.

"Genevieve," Nick said, coming up behind her. Wrapping his arms around her, he gently turned her away from the scene. Urging her into the shelter of his arms, he held her tight. "I'm so sorry."

Stroking his hands up and down her back, he murmured, "I watched the feed on my way over. So pissed. Because there was nothing I could do but watch as he popped open the safe like it was nothing and took everything you'd worked so hard for."

"You saw the video? Clearly? It was him?"

"No mistake at all. I'm going to turn it over to the police, although I'm not sure they'll need it. You saw. They caught him with some of your pieces in his pockets."

The sick, hollow sensation spread from her belly to her chest. The show. "I need to see."

She needed irrefutable proof.

Pulling free, Genevieve spun on her heel, heading straight for the front door. A gentleman there attempted to detain her, until she explained the studio was hers.

Walking inside was like waking up in the middle of a nightmare. The heavy safe doors stood wide open. A couple of her pieces spilled over the edge of the drawers. But she could see where the settings had been snapped.

Swallowing the lump in her throat, Genevieve refused to cry. It wouldn't do any good. She needed to assess the damage and see if there was anything salvageable.

Her equipment had been moved, tables pushed out of place and a couple chairs overturned. Picking her way through the rubble, she pulled open the drawers in the safe, one after the other, devastated at what she found.

Dropping to a crouch, she pressed the heels of her hands against her stinging eyes.

Nick's hand landed on her back. She knew he was trying to give her support, but right now, the last thing she wanted was to be touched.

But because she knew he meant well, she didn't shake him off.

"It's ruined. Everything," she finally croaked out. Her mind spun. In a matter of days, she was going to be in breach of contract with Mitchell Brothers. Legitimately, they could come after her for everything she had. They'd sunk a lot of resources into the release of her collection and in anticipation of selling the pieces in all their stores for the Christmas shopping season.

She had nothing to give them.

"I'm ruined." The words were out of her mouth before she realized they'd formed in her mind. "What am I going to do? How am I going to provide for Noah?"

Goddamn Finn!

"Why? Why would he do this? He doesn't need the money. Hell, he doesn't even need the challenge. It doesn't make sense."

Nick's fingers squeezed her shoulder. "Who knows how the man thinks? He's never needed the money from the things he's stolen. You know that's not why he does it. He's sick. He has a compulsion he can't control."

No, that wasn't true. Although Finn's words from several days ago rang in her ears. He went to Stone, *itchy*, he'd said. Stone had provided him a legitimate outlet.

Maybe it hadn't been enough?

But why *destroy* her pieces? She could understand Finn taking them—no, *understand* was the wrong word. She could have dealt with him taking them. But ripping her work apart?

It made no sense. He had nothing to gain from doing

that. He'd bought three of her pieces, dammit. What purpose would this serve?

None that she could think of.

But the evidence was hard to ignore. And she'd always said Finn DeLuca had a purpose for everything he did. Maybe she just didn't have all the pieces yet to understand.

Slowly, Nick folded down so he was crouched beside her. Looking her straight in the eye, a sad expression pulling against the corners of his eyes, he said, "As much as I hate to say it, maybe it's time you called your grandfather. He could help you."

Oh, wouldn't Lackland simply love that.

The memory of his sneer and disparaging words from the gala ran through her head. When she'd left to live on her own, she'd promised herself that no circumstance existed where she'd go back. Not only did she deserve better than the toxic, abusive environment her grandfather created, but so did her son.

Unfortunately, her son also needed to eat and have a roof over his head. And if Mitchell came after her for what they could…even those basic necessities were in jeopardy.

Once again, she'd been naive. Obviously, there was a circumstance where she would go back to her grandfather.

Providing for her son would be worth anything, including subjecting herself to that environment.

Lackland was going to relish not only that she was crawling back, begging. But that she was doing it after Finn had ruined her.

Again.

* * *

Genevieve stared at the phone sitting on the kitchen table in front of her. She'd spent hours at the studio, evaluating exactly where she was and speaking with the officers.

After viewing the video Nick showed her…it was difficult to remain hopeful that there was an explanation.

While she hadn't seen his face—because he wouldn't be that sloppy—Finn had made one mistake. The shadowy figure had been wearing the same clothes Finn had been when he'd run out the front door of her studio, her jewels stuffed in his pockets.

There were two phone calls she needed to make, both of which she was dreading. Mitchell Brothers and her grandfather.

If there was one thing Lackland had taught her, it was to get the task you were dreading the most out of the way first.

Snatching up the phone, Genevieve flicked open the screen and quickly scrolled to her contacts. And the number she'd hoped never to need again.

Hitting the button, she dialed her grandfather, dread and disappointment churning in her belly.

"Genevieve."

Even the sound of his voice made her want to vomit.

"I hear you've had some excitement today."

Of course he'd heard. Her grandfather made sure he was aware of everything important that happened in the city.

"Yes."

"Such a shame your collection with Mitchell has been ruined."

He didn't even attempt to hide the pure glee filling his voice.

Genevieve desperately wished she could tell him that everything was going to be fine. That she had the situation well in hand. But she didn't. And years of dealing with the man had taught her, it was easier to keep her words simple and short. To let him gloat and believe he'd won. It made the unpleasant experience end faster.

And right now, that's what she wanted. To get through this conversation so she could take the next steps forward.

"I assume you're contacting me, for the first time in three years, to ask for my assistance."

Genevieve gritted her teeth, wishing she could keep the word behind her teeth. Unfortunately, that couldn't happen. "Yes."

"Hmm. I wonder, my dear, if you remember my words when you left, pregnant and disgraced?"

Of course she remembered his words. He'd been bitter and mean. Telling her that she was destined to fail at any attempt to be self-sufficient because she was stupid, incompetent and untrustworthy.

But it wouldn't matter what she said at this point. Lackland was going to delight in reminding her. No doubt that was part of what he was most looking forward to.

"I told you that you'd fail on your own. No matter what, you'd manage to screw things up and would need to come crawling back to me."

"Yes, Grandfather."

"And here we are. Exactly where I said you'd be."

Genevieve closed her eyes and waited for him to make his demands, because there was no denying that he would.

"And if I remember correctly, I promised you that I wouldn't lift a hand to help you at that point."

Of course he had, but Genevieve knew he'd never stick by that statement. Not when he had the perfect opportunity to have her back under his thumb, a puppet he could control.

Her grandfather liked nothing more than controlling people.

"However, three years is a long time and perhaps I was a bit hasty back then. I'd welcome you back into the family and at Reilly, but I have a few demands."

Of course he did. Genevieve had expected nothing less.

"I refuse to accept the son of that thief as my great-grandson."

Genevieve sat straight up in her chair. What exactly was he saying?

"However, I recognize that he's your son. So, I'm willing to accept you back on the condition that your son is sent to boarding school. Your focus should be on Reilly and the designs you'll be creating for our company, anyway."

No, there was no way Genevieve would ever agree to send her toddler to boarding school. "He's not even three yet," she ground out.

"I'm aware. I'm certain I can find a school willing

to accept him despite his age. Better he grow up in that environment, anyway. The sooner he realizes that he's alone in the world and won't be accepted as part of this family, the better."

She wanted to scream. She wanted to cry. She wanted to curse both her grandfather and Finn for putting her in this position.

Lackland didn't even wait to hear her response. "Those are my terms. Take them or leave them," he said, before cutting the connection.

The dial tone buzzed through Genevieve's head, along with anger and despair.

Fourteen

Genevieve pulled Noah tight into her arms. Her son squirmed, pushing against her, wanting down so he could toddle over to the pile of toys in the corner and play.

He was completely innocent and oblivious to everything going on around him. To the changes that could potentially rock his world.

Genevieve set Noah on his feet, and he didn't even look back at her before tearing across the room. If she did go back to her grandfather—and that was a big if—she'd find some way around her grandfather's demand.

She had to.

Luckily, she didn't have to make that decision tonight. Or even tomorrow. The Mitchell brothers had generously given her a few days to figure everything out and evaluate what could be salvaged.

Right now, her focus was Noah. Partly because that was easy.

"Noah, you want some chicken nuggets?" The thought of food might make her stomach turn, but her son still needed to eat.

Abandoning his toys, Noah shot back across the room. Bumping into her knees, he wrapped his arms around her legs and looked up at her with a huge smile on his face.

Chicken nuggets were his favorite.

"Dinosaws?" he asked.

"Of course. Go play. I'll get them ready."

Confident she was going to get him what he needed, her son went back to his toys. Genevieve went into the kitchen. Keeping an eye on him, she pulled the bag from the freezer and preheated the oven.

The moment was normal and domestic. Something she'd done hundreds of times. But right now, it felt wrong. Because she shouldn't be doing it alone.

She'd just popped the pan into the oven when there was a loud knock on her door.

With a sigh, Genevieve dropped her head and squeezed her eyes tight. She wasn't in the mood to deal with anyone, not even well-meaning friends. She'd already called Nicole to say she wasn't going into the studio tonight.

Standing in the middle of her kitchen, Genevieve contemplated ignoring the knock. Everything inside her balked at the idea of being impolite, but she really didn't have the energy to deal.

Honestly, she was afraid that at the first well-meaning

word from anyone's mouth she was going to lose it. Right now, she was holding it together for Noah.

But when the polite knock morphed into an insistent pounding that rattled her front door, Genevieve decided it would be easier to open the door and pointedly tell whoever was there to go the hell away.

Whether she would have actually said that or not was a moot point because when she opened the door, she was shocked silent.

Anderson Stone asked, "Can we come in?" but didn't bother waiting for her answer before scooting by her into the foyer.

The man with him followed silently behind, pausing long enough to shut her front door with a quiet click. It didn't take a genius to figure out this was probably Gray Lockwood, the third musketeer.

Shaken from her stupor, her words dripped with sarcasm as she swept an arm wide indicating her den. "Make yourselves at home."

Stone gave her a long look before the corner of his mouth quirked up into a little grin. "Look at that, the mild-mannered thing has teeth."

"I don't know what you want or why you're here, but I'm really not in the mood right now."

For the first time, Gray spoke. "You're going to want to see this, I promise."

His voice was smooth and deep. For some reason it made her think of smoke-filled rooms with brocade wallpaper and filigreed sconces. A twenties speakeasy with gangsters, beautiful women and rich Scotch.

Blond and polished, he was the contrast to Finn's

swarthy, mischievous demeanor. He was also quieter
and less assuming than Stone, who always seemed to
be up front and in charge.

Not that she particularly cared, but staring at the
two men standing in her den, she wondered how the
prison they'd been in had survived all three of them.
At once. They were gorgeous, cunning and autocratic.
Together, she had no doubt they'd been a force to be
reckoned with.

They still were.

Turning her attention to Gray, she asked, "What do
I need to see?"

Walking into the kitchen and over to the table, Gray
set down a laptop she hadn't even noticed he'd been
holding. Popping it open, he clicked a few buttons and
began playing a video. Stepping back, he waved her
forward so she could get a better look.

A frown pulling at her mouth, she did as he'd indi-
cated. It took her several moments to orient herself to
what she was watching. Some context might have been
helpful, but probably would have blunted the impact of
the images on the screen.

The video was perfectly clear, no doubt because the
men standing behind her could afford to buy state-of-
the-art equipment. But that didn't negate the fact that
it had obviously been dark whenever the footage was
taken.

Despite that, it was easy to identify Nick and her
grandfather leaning close and engaging in an intense
conversation.

She didn't need to hear the words being spoken to

know that Lackland Reilly was pissed. Mostly because she'd been the recipient of the expression on numerous occasions.

Nick wasn't exactly happy, either, but he was clearly deferring to her grandfather.

Genevieve understood what she was looking at, but not the implications Gray and Stone were obviously trying to make. She needed more information. Turning, her gaze bounced between the two men as she asked, "What is this? When was it taken? What are they talking about?"

Before they could answer, Noah came bouncing into the kitchen. He gave both men a cursory glance before making a beeline for Genevieve.

"'Saws?"

She'd completely forgotten about the nuggets in the oven. "Yes, baby. I'll get them out."

Making a move around the men, she started into the kitchen, but Stone stopped her. A hand on her arm, he said, "I'll get it. Let Gray explain."

She watched as one of the wealthiest men in the South scooped her son up, lifted Noah over his head and plopped him down onto his shoulders. Noah squealed, wrapping his chubby fingers in Stone's hair.

She watched Stone's tight grip around her son's back, holding him securely in place. Twisting his head so he could talk up at her son, he said, "Your daddy asked me to keep an eye on you while he's gone for a little bit. Let's get you those nuggets, little man."

Watching the scene before her, it was difficult to reconcile the elegant man in the expensive suit she'd met just a few days ago with the one letting her toddler's diaper-clad rear bounce up and down against his shoulders as they went to get chicken nuggets out of her oven.

"Cut them up into little pieces and make sure they're not hot enough to burn his mouth," Genevieve said, a little bemused.

Stone tossed her a big grin. "We got this, Momma. Listen to Gray."

Gray took that as his cue. Tapping a few keys on the computer, he pulled up another video feed and pressed Play. A man of few words, he again didn't bother to tell her what she was about to watch.

The screen was split between two feeds, both of which were of her studio. One camera was clearly pointed directly at her safe, although she'd never seen footage from this angle. The other had a wide view of her back door and the hallway leading into the workroom.

"Finn asked us to set up a couple additional cameras that he didn't mention to you or Nick."

"Why?"

Why would he do that? So he could have access to watch the studio that no one else was aware of? But, obviously, *someone* had been aware of it since Gray was showing her the feed.

His friends had been in on the plan the entire time. That was surely the more logical explanation. However, that didn't explain why they were both in her house right now.

Unless they were upset that all their hard work had

yielded nothing and were hoping to play some other angle.

God, Genevieve was confused. And conflicted. None of this made any sense. Both of the men in her home had enough to money to buy everything she owned, including the jewels Finn had attempted to steal.

Hell, *Finn* had enough money to buy everything she owned.

And that's what she kept circling around in her brain. None of this made sense.

So she watched the feed, trying to find some clue that would answer all the questions that kept swirling inside her head.

It took her several moments to realize a dark shadow was lurking in the hallway by her back door. As she watched, it shifted and flowed into her workroom. Her eyes immediately jumped to the second half of the screen, waiting to see what would happen next.

The slim shape paused in front of her safe. The doors quickly swung open. "That was fast."

Gray hummed, "Almost as if someone had the code."

She'd given Finn a lot of access, but she hadn't shared the code for the safe with him. Mostly because it hadn't occurred to her that she'd need to and he hadn't asked for it. But he had been in the room when she'd opened it on several occasions. He was smart and observant enough to memorize it if he'd wanted to.

She expected to see the shadow reach inside and start taking pieces. But that's not what happened. Instead, the person pulled out a tool, the metal glinting for a moment through the darkness, and began systematically ripping her pieces apart.

That had been bothering her from the very beginning. The stones were valuable, but they were already set. Why destroy the pieces? It wasn't like any of them were notorious—like the Star of Reilly—or would be difficult to fence just as they were. Perhaps down the road it would make sense to separate the stones so they'd be more difficult to trace, but why take the time to do it in the middle of stealing them?

She didn't understand.

But then, she wasn't a thief. So maybe Finn had a reason?

Her confusion thickened, though, when the thief took a handful of the gems and sprinkled them across the floor and her worktable like a trail of bread crumbs from a fairy tale.

Then, without taking a single stone, the shadow slipped back out into the hallway. And waited.

What was frustrating was that, even though the surveillance equipment was high quality and the feed clear, the person managed to keep their face hidden by twisting and melting into the shadows.

But that wouldn't be difficult to do for someone who knew where every camera was placed.

"What's he waiting for?" Genevieve finally asked, after staring for a couple minutes at footage of the thief simply standing there.

"Wait."

Suddenly, the shadow moved. Fast. Darting back through the hallway and into the workroom. This time, he didn't stop at the safe, but ran through, knocking over one of the tables, pulling a rolling table with equipment out into the middle of the room and overturning a couple chairs before racing into the front.

At the same time, motion at the back door caught her attention. Turning her focus, Genevieve let out a gasp when Finn came through. He wasn't even bothering to hide his face from the cameras. Instead, he was intent on getting into her workroom as quickly as possible.

She watched him survey the damage. His body jerked, as if he'd been punched, and his mouth moved, although she couldn't hear what he said. She could guess, though.

Racing through, he stopped long enough to scoop up several of the jewels scattered across the floor, stuffing them into the pockets of his pants. He took the same path as the shadow, pushing chairs, table and equipment out of his way.

The feed cut off, but Genevieve continued to stare at the blank screen for several moments, her mind spinning.

Could they have doctored the footage?

She absolutely believed they had the expertise and equipment to do it. But to what end? What did Stone and Gray have to gain from showing this to her?

Other than freeing Finn.

But what did any of them have to gain from stealing her pieces? No, from destroying them?

Nothing. That was the logical answer.

Which left her with the question, who did have something to gain?

Turning slowly, she faced Gray. Arms crossed over his chest, he'd simply been standing and waiting.

"Explain what I just watched, please."

A frown pulled his brows into a tight V. "Finn didn't break in and steal from you."

"Obviously. I mean, what else? Who did break in?" She had no doubt Gray and Stone knew more about what was going on than they were saying. They might be keeping it to themselves because they weren't certain what her reaction would be, but they were going to have to get over that. "Why did you show me the first video and what does it have to do with everything else?"

"Finn asked us to put Nick under surveillance. He's had Lackland watched since before he got out of prison."

Later she'd address why he'd felt the need to do that—and not mention it—but right now it was immaterial.

"How long?"

"Almost a year."

About the time Gray had been released and several months before Stone and Finn. She'd done her research on all three once she'd realized who they were to him.

"It wasn't until the last few weeks, though, that we placed Nick under the same scrutiny. Or learned that he met with Lackland. It's possible—probable—they communicated the whole time. We simply can't prove it."

"What can you prove?"

Gray reached over and began clicking a few keys, shutting off the computer. He didn't look at her as he said, "What you probably suspect. Nick has been giving your grandfather information. He's also been working with him the last few weeks to sabotage the release of your collection. Reilly is hurting. The last few collections they've released haven't performed as well as anticipated. Competition from companies like Mitchell Brothers hasn't helped. Your grandfather has been leveraging assets to maintain his lavish lifestyle, anticipating the market would bounce back."

"Which hasn't happened." Genevieve was fully aware of the reputation Reilly had. The company was known for being old-fashioned. However, that wasn't always a bad thing. It also maintained a reputation for quality and excellence. "I didn't realize."

"No one does. He's worked hard to keep the truth from the board. The problems started about the time you left."

Which made sense. Up until that point, she'd been the one designing collections, for both their major commercial clients as well as any VIPs.

Genevieve stared at Gray for several moments, letting everything sink in.

"Finn didn't do anything wrong." Relief flooded through her.

Finn hadn't done anything wrong. She'd been right to question the evidence in front of her.

She should have trusted him. Trusted her own instincts more. She owed Finn a huge apology. And she needed to stop questioning his motives and trust he only had her and Noah's best interests at heart.

She simply wasn't used to anyone else caring enough about her to place her needs first. Or hell, second or third.

"Nope, he didn't do anything wrong."

"I heard that cop. They're not going to listen when he tells them the truth."

"Nope."

"I assume you're going to use this to prove he's right?" Genevieve asked, waving her hand at the computer on the table beside them.

"Yep."

"I want to come with you. I want to be there when they let him go."

Gray nodded. "You realize this implicates Nick and your grandfather. I have other evidence I plan to turn over."

"Good."

"They're both going to prison, but the police will want you to press charges."

"Happy to."

"Nick's been one of your closest friends for the last several years."

"Apparently not." Genevieve's face scrunched into a frown. "Are you trying to talk me out of doing this? Do you think it matters to me? My grandfather is a despicable man and always has been. And if Nick let him influence his choices, then he has to deal with the consequences."

In the kitchen, Noah's peel of laughter pulled her attention for several seconds. Watching her son, light filling his perfect face, her chest tightened.

"Despite everything, I love Finn. Sometimes I think I shouldn't, but I can't help it. He's charismatic, charming and mischievous. He has this uncanny ability to draw people to him. And more importantly, he recognizes strength inside of me when I can't see it for myself."

Gray's hand on her shoulder startled her. His gaze was steady and calm when Genevieve looked back to him. This man had deep wells of patience and understanding. The intelligence behind his eyes would have been intimidating if his demeanor wasn't so calm and assured.

"I know."

A relieved smile curled her lips. "So let's go save his impulsive ass."

Fifteen

Finn stared at the blank walls of the cell and tried not to let claustrophobia win.

He'd been grilled for the last several hours. Rapid-fire questions designed to trip him up and poke holes in his story. Unfortunately for the investigators, his story was solid. Because it was the truth.

Not that they'd been willing to listen.

They were still convinced he was lying. And based on several of the questions they asked him, their conviction was supported by something more than what had happened at Genevieve's studio. Obviously, they weren't revealing their information to him, but from what he could piece together, it had something to do with Hunt.

He needed to get in touch with Stone to clear up this whole mess. But what he needed more was to speak with

Genevieve. Although from the expression on her face, he wasn't sure she'd be willing to listen to anything he had to say, either.

How was he about to lose everything when he hadn't done a damn thing wrong?

For the first time in his life, he'd attempted to follow the rules. And everything was turning to shit. Only learning of Sawyer's death had ever left him feeling this hopeless and helpless.

He'd spent the last few weeks proving to Genevieve that he'd changed. He'd made an effort to earn her trust, and he'd been certain those efforts were paying off.

Apparently not.

At the first sign of trouble, she'd believed the worst. She didn't question what was happening or whether he was innocent. She definitely hadn't offered her support. From the devastation on her face, it was clear she'd believed he'd stolen from her.

Which hurt most of all.

Finn had no doubt that eventually, with Stone and Gray's help, he would clear up the misunderstanding.

But he could see now that no matter how straight and narrow he attempted to live his life, it would never be enough. Genevieve would always be waiting for him to screw up.

And even if he deserved it, he couldn't live his life that way.

Rubbing a hand over his tight chest, Finn wanted to scream and throw something. But everything in the cell was bolted down.

Dropping his head back against the wall, he shut his

eyes and let his body sag. Bone-deep exhaustion pulled at every muscle.

He had no idea how long he sat in the cell, but a while later an officer showed up outside. The door slid open and he gestured for Finn to follow.

"You know, it doesn't matter how many times you ask the questions, my answers aren't changing. I didn't steal anything."

The officer frowned at him. "This time."

Leading him through the sterilized hallways, it took Finn a few seconds to register what he'd actually said. "What do you mean, this time?"

"We know you didn't take anything from Ms. Reilly. All charges have been dropped."

"They have?" Finn tried not to sound incredulous, but failed. This was too easy.

Or maybe it wasn't. He'd assumed it would be morning before Stone could get things straightened out, but maybe he'd worked a bit faster.

That had to be it.

The officer led him to a woman, who processed his release. She gave him back the personal belongings that had been cataloged when they'd booked him. And then directed him through double doors and out of the station.

Freedom was a beautiful thing.

Until he walked out and found Genevieve waiting for him on the other side.

The sight of him was overwhelming.

Genevieve didn't realize just how scared she'd been

until he pushed through those doors. She wanted to rush over and grab him. Put her hands on him and make sure he was there and unharmed.

But she didn't deserve that yet and wasn't sure what her reception would be. He definitely hadn't greeted her with his mischievous, open smile. She moved closer anyway, unable to stay away from him.

She wanted to reach for him, but stopped herself. Instead, she led with, "I'm sorry."

It hurt that he didn't reach for her, either. He stood in front of her, his expression shuttered and remote in a way that left a pit in her belly. "For what?"

"Doubting you, even for a little while. I realized nothing made sense pretty quickly, before Stone and Gray came to me. But I let my doubt and fears convince me that you must have done *something*."

His voice was flat when he said, "It's okay."

"It isn't."

"You know what? You're right. It isn't. I've changed who I am for you and Noah, Genevieve. I've given up a piece of me. After Sawyer died, I turned to stealing as a way of blocking out the pain, but also reminding myself of just how shitty a person I could really be. Good people don't steal."

Genevieve stepped closer. "Stop. You're a good person, Finn. One of the best men I've ever met."

"Bullshit. The expression on your face when they put me in that cop car said everything. You don't believe that. And no matter what I do, you never will."

"That's not true." She took another step, trying to bridge the distance between them in more ways than one. "You deserve my faith. Not simply because you've earned it, but because deep down I know the man you are. I *know* you have a code of honor you live by. It might not be the same one everyone else follows, but it's hard and fast for you. Unshakable. Even discounting the fact that you don't want or need anything I own, you'd never hurt me. Or use me. You're right. I should have trusted you. But I'm human, too, Finn. And I made a mistake."

Finn stared at her for several seconds. Genevieve had no idea what was going on behind his closed expression. Which scared the crap out of her.

But finally, Finn moved. Closing the gap between them, he ran the pads of his fingers across her cheek. "God, I can't stay mad at you, no matter how much I know I should. Of course I'd never hurt you or Noah. You two have become everything to me."

Leaning into his caress, Genevieve soaked up the warmth of his palm against her skin.

His mouth twisted. "I've given you reason to question me. I recognize that. Regret it every single day."

Shaking her head, Genevieve wrapped her fingers in the soft fabric of his shirt and tugged him closer. "It's not fair to continue to punish you for a single mistake that you've acknowledged, apologized for and done everything you could to atone for. That's all I can ask of you."

But it was more than that. "By every word and action, you've shown nothing but support for me. You accept me exactly as I am. Want my happiness and success. You're an amazing father to our son. We're both lucky to have you in our lives."

Slipping her hands up his chest, Genevieve cradled them around his jaw. "I love you, Finn. I have since the moment I met you. You're dynamic, challenging and the most accepting person I've ever met. You don't always make it easy—"

Finn laughed, the sound coming out a little strangled.

"—but you do make it worth it. You put up a good front, pretend to be this wicked soul, but deep down you're a good man with a beautiful heart."

She would have said more, but suddenly she was crushed against Finn's body. His mouth was on hers, kissing the hell out of her. The moment was filled with heat and promise. Someone behind them cleared their throat. Another person whistled.

Genevieve didn't care.

She was out of breath when he finally pulled back, murmuring against her lips, "Hush, woman. Give a guy the chance to say I love you, too."

Finn stared deep into her eyes. "I don't know what I did to deserve you and Noah, but I plan to spend the rest of my life appreciating the gift I've been given. I can't promise I'll never screw up."

Genevieve couldn't stop a huff of laughter. "I have no doubt." They were confessing their love in the middle of a *police station*, after all.

"I can promise I'll always put you and our family first. And I'll do everything in my power to protect that. Working with Stone and Gray will help."

This was the one thing that worried her. But she had

to place her trust in Finn. "Just promise that if it's ever not enough you'll talk to me. I won't judge, Finn. I want to give you the same level of support you've shown me."

"That's an easy promise to make."

Pulling her in, Finn kissed her again. Genevieve let out a sigh, of happiness, relief and pure joy.

Wrapping an arm around her shoulders, Finn turned to lead her out of the station. "Let's go home to our son."

Epilogue

Finn hung back, watching Genevieve. She stood in the middle of the conference room, her gaze wandering around the empty space.

He knew she was nervous because they'd talked about it this morning, but he also had no doubt she was going to be the best CEO Reilly International ever had.

Her grandfather and Nick had both been arrested. In exchange for a reduced sentence, Nick had testified against Lackland, explaining her grandfather's intricate plan to ruin Genevieve and leave her no choice but to crawl back to him and Reilly. They'd both spend several years behind bars. As far as Finn was concerned, that wasn't enough time for what they'd attempted to do to Genevieve, but no one had asked him.

Her grandfather's arrest had left a hole at Reilly.

After much discussion, the board had voted her in as CEO. After several protests, Genevieve had agreed to take the position, as long as it was understood her focus would be on designing.

She was going to kick butt. She had a lot of hard work ahead of her to bring the company back from the brink, but everyone had faith in her ability to do it.

The Mitchell brothers had been understanding, allowing her time to re-create the pieces Nick had destroyed. The collection launch had been pushed back and they'd missed the Christmas window, but in the end it hadn't mattered. Publicity had been wonderful and the collection was selling well. Not only that, but Genevieve was already speaking to them about a partnership with Reilly.

People slowly started trickling into the room, including Stone and Gray. She'd consulted with both men before agreeing to take on the role of CEO. Finn wasn't entirely certain what had happened while he was being questioned, but whatever it was had brought the three most important people in his life together.

Genevieve trusted Stone and Gray, and given their business backgrounds, Finn thought it was a great idea to use them as resources while she figured out how to run the company.

Hanging at the back of the room, Finn wasn't surprised when Stone and Gray slid up on either side of him.

The side-eye they gave him had him asking, "What've I done now?"

"Nothing," Stone said, a little too quickly.

"Then what do you want?"

"Nothing," Gray answered.

Nope, Finn wasn't buying it. "Bullshit."

Shrugging, Stone said, "We're just wondering how long it's going to take you to convince her to marry you."

Finn twisted, looking from one to the other. A knowing smirk played at the corners of Stone's mouth. He had to fight hard against the urge to smack it off. Gray, on the other hand, simply stared straight ahead. His expression grim and remote as usual.

"You guys are hilarious."

Stone's eyes danced. "She doesn't have any family. We're just looking out for her."

This was going to be fun. "For your information, we got married last week."

That got a reaction out of both of them. "Wait. What?"

"With everything going on, she didn't want a big event. And the moment we realized she was pregnant again, I wanted my ring on her finger."

Gray leaned sideways, looking around the people milling in the room. "Which she still doesn't have."

"Oh, she has it. We're waiting until after today to make the announcement."

"Pregnant, huh?" Stone clapped him on the back. "Congratulations, man. On both counts. You deserve to be happy."

"Until I met Genevieve, I wasn't sure I did." Finn couldn't fight the blooming smile. "But I'm not going to question it, I'm simply going to accept it and enjoy."

"Amen, brother," Stone drawled his agreement.

In unison, he and Stone turned to look at Gray. Their friend didn't even shift his attention as he responded, "Don't even go there."

"Any movement on your end?"

Gray's eyes narrowed, crinkling at the edges. "As a matter of fact…there is. With any luck, I'll have some new information in a few weeks."

"That's great news," Finn said. "Anything you need, you let us know."

Gray nodded, murmuring something under his breath that sounded strangely like *bail money*.

But before Finn could ask, the board meeting was called to order. There'd be plenty of time to interrogate his friend later and figure out just what was going on with Gray. Now that Finn and Stone were settled, it was long past time to focus on getting Gray's life back for him.

Together, they were going to solve the mystery and figure out just who had framed Gray.

* * * * *

Look for Gray's story,
The Sinner's Secret
Available November 2020

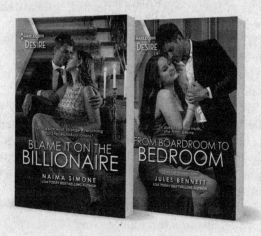

COMING NEXT MONTH FROM

HARLEQUIN

DESIRE

Available November 3, 2020

#2767 CLAIMING THE RANCHER'S HEIR

Gold Valley Vineyards • by Maisey Yates

It's Christmas and rancher Creed Cooper must work with his rival, Wren Maxfield—so tempers flare! But animosity becomes passion and, now, Wren is pregnant. Creed wants a marriage in name only. But as desire takes over, this may be a vow neither can keep...

#2768 IN BED WITH HIS RIVAL

Texas Cattleman's Club: Rags to Riches

by Katherine Garbera

With a bitter legal battle between their families, lawyer Brian Cooper knows he should stay away from Piper Holloway. For Piper, having a fling with a younger man is fun...until stunning truths are revealed. Now can she ever trust him with her heart?

#2769 SLOW BURN

Dynasties: Seven Sins • by Janice Maynard

Jake Lowell has been a globe-trotting playboy for years, ignoring all his family obligations. Until he learns his one hot night with hardworking Nikki Reardon resulted in a child. Will his history threaten a future with the woman who got away?

#2770 VOWS IN NAME ONLY

Billionaires of Boston • by Naima Simone

When CEO Cain Farrell is blackmailed into marrying his enemy's daughter, he vows it will be a marriage on paper only. But one sizzling kiss with Devon Cole changes everything. Can he look past her father's sins to build a real future together?

#2771 THE SINNER'S SECRET

Bad Billionaires • by Kira Sinclair

Wrongly convicted executive Gray Lockwood will stop at nothing to prove his innocence, including working with the woman who put him behind bars, accountant Blakely Whittaker. But now this billionaire realizes he doesn't just want justice, he wants her...

#2772 ALL HE WANTS FOR CHRISTMAS

The Sterling Wives • by Karen Booth

Andrew Sterling wants one thing: to destroy his dead brother's company. But when his brother's widow, Miranda, invites Andrew over for the holidays, attraction ignites. He'll have to choose between the woman in his bed and the resentment that has guided him until now...

"Come here," he said, his voice suddenly hard. "I want to show you something."

There was a big white tent that was still closed, reserved for an evening hors d'oeuvre session for people who had bought premium tickets, and he compelled her inside. It was already set up with tables and tablecloths, everything elegant and dainty, and exceedingly Maxfield. Though there were bottles of Cowboy Wines on each table, along with bottles of Maxfield select.

But they were not apparently here to look at the wine, or indeed anything else that was set up. Which she discovered when he cupped her chin with firm fingers and looked directly into her eyes.

"I've done nothing but think about you for two weeks. I want you. Not just something hot and quick against a wall. I need you in a bed, Wren. We need some time to explore this. To explore each other."

She blinked. She had not expected that.

He'd been avoiding her and she'd been so sure it was because he didn't want this.

But he was here in a suit.

And he had a look of intent gleaming in those green eyes.

She realized then she'd gotten it all wrong.

"I...I agree."

She also hadn't expected to agree.

"I want you now," she whispered, and before she could stop herself, she was up on her tiptoes and kissing that infuriating mouth.

She wanted to sigh with relief. She had been so angry at him. So angry at the way he had ignored this. Because how dare he? He had never ignored the anger between them. No. He had taken every opportunity to goad and prod her in anger. So why, why had he ignored this?

But he hadn't.

They were devouring each other, and neither of them cared that there were people outside. His large hands palmed her ass, pulling her up against his body so she could feel just how hard he was for her. She arched against him, gasping when the center of her need came into contact with his rampant masculinity.

She didn't understand the feelings she had for this man. Where everything about him that she found so disturbing was also the very thing that drove her into his arms.

Too big. Too rough. Crass. Untamable. He was everything she detested, everything she desired.

All that, and he was distracting her from an event that she had planned. Which was a cardinal sin in her book. And she didn't even care.

He set her away from him suddenly, breaking their kiss. "Not now," he said, his voice rough. "Tonight. All night. You. In my bed."

Don't miss what happens next in...
Claiming the Rancher's Heir
by New York Times *bestselling author Maisey Yates!*

Available November 2020 wherever
Harlequin Desire books and ebooks are sold.

Harlequin.com

Get 4 FREE REWARDS!

We'll send you 2 FREE Books plus 2 FREE Mystery Gifts.

Harlequin Desire® books transport you to the world of the American elite with juicy plot twists, delicious sensuality and intriguing scandal.

FREE Value Over $20